Beneath *the* Sycamore Tree

MONTIE APOSTOLOS

PAGE PUBLISHING, INC.
Conneaut Lake, PA

First originally published by Page Publishing 2021

ISBN 978-1-6624-4311-4 (pbk)
ISBN 978-1-6624-4312-1 (digital)

Printed in the United States of America

Dedicated to my two lovely granddaughters Jessica Lauren and Marisa Nicole whose strength I draw from in writing this novel. Thanks for allowing me into that space that permits me to see you through the lens of unconditional love.

To my daughter Kemyata who granted me the opportunity to become a grandparent, raising them to love God first and with the notion to enjoy life to its fullest. To God for the three gifts He granted me in this space.

Contents

Author's Summary

BENEATH THE SYCAMORE Tree spans from the 1960s to 1980s. It chronicles the life of a young black girl from a middle-class family in Jackson, Mississippi, who through her relationship with her grandmother decides that dreams do not have to be deferred. It is an emotional journey as she travels the world taking risks to find what it takes to become successful, but more importantly, she discovers love in the process with an unlikely and often forbidden lover and friend.

I relied on my own personal experiences growing up in writing this literary piece exploring a rich understanding of racism and its impact. The ignorance and preconceived attitudes the protagonist experienced or her family felt are all experiences I can speak to as an African American woman. I am a product of the South during the tried and tested '50s and '60s. My godfather was a famous civil rights leader. As a black person, my tested growth led me to have and relish a defining relationship with my grandmother. My family's experience with classicism but more importantly racism catapulted me to the mindset that in order to transform the collective, we must be willing to broach racism in industries that perpetuate it and social norms that perpetuate it as well. Lisa's life decisions spoke to the human condition. She, however, refused to be boxed in. In the 1960s and 1980s, this was unheard of as a norm for black people and specifically black women.

This novel is unique because it exposes the reader to and defies stereotypes about people of color such as being poor and uneducated during the era of segregation. The protagonist comes from a middle-class black family (not sheltered from the ills of racism), but her story could be any young girl's story that is seeking to discover who she is and any young woman who may be trying to break the glass ceiling. Lisa takes this journey but not without events that challenge her to remember the intrinsic value in the lessons she learned from her grandmother beneath the sycamore tree.

Beneath the Sycamore Tree shows the world that black families can become successful through opportunities and hard and smart work. More importantly, it is a desire to break the mold as well as barriers that have sometime perpetuated a fixed mindset about the black community; that success is often a distant dream. It also shows us a world in which attitudes of racism and prejudice would not deter the destiny of a little black girl because she believed in herself and her grandmother's words that she could be whomever she wanted to become. This derived from dialogue beneath the sycamore tree.

Chapter 1

In the Beginning

THERE IS MUCH to be learned beneath the sycamore tree. I found comfort in the strength of the tree. While symbolic of the life I had lived, the deciduous tree was always where I could feel safe and free. I had much to feel safe about from the years of learning to love myself and learning to be without love in order to accomplish that feat. I was born and raised in the South in Jackson, Mississippi, during the turbulent '50s and '60s, a time when during summers, you could fry an egg on the sidewalk sunny-side up. I was born where people didn't talk about much because they just wanted to experience life precariously. Quiet moments in your thoughts were treated like diamonds. Although you could not ignore that life had something else going on in the wings that begged for your attention. A race of people crying for respect and equality would not be ignored. I lived on Prosperity Street. What irony since we were not rich, but I never felt poor. I left home at the age of eighteen primarily because I needed to recover from the psychological, physical, and sexual abuse I endured from the age of nine years old from a family friend. Sometimes I had to fight my way through the room when his old ass was visiting. He would hide his ass around a corner and jump out. "Girl, you show look mature these days, wha yo daddy feeding you?" I would roll my eyes and rush through before he could ever open his mouth again, which by the way had rotten teeth. His breathe smelled of liquor, and I'm sure his ass did too. Johnny Ray purported to be intelligent. You know, the type who stands around trying to tell everybody what's going on in society. He was an "Ur rah." Ask him a question…or not, and to show how intelligent he was or tried to be, he would start his sentence speaking proper with "Ur rah." I also left home because I had been given wings to fly to heights that had been set by my parents, Granny, and ultimately me.

In 1966, when I was nine years old, my mother died of cancer. Before she died, I was not sure if my father ever understood what he really had in her, or perhaps he knew but regretted that the ravaging disease would rob her of realizing it herself. She was tall and lanky; she had long hair as black as coal. When she walked past you, could smell the lavender talcum powder she wore or the soap if she had just gotten out of the tub. She wore these sleek cotton dresses that stuck to her like a glove on a hot summer day, showing every curve she had. Her teeth were as white as cotton, and her lips were full and plump, so beautifully pronounced. She was very soft-spoken, and her puppy eyes and bright smile would hypnotize you into doing the right thing. I had a great relationship with my mother, maybe even a little overprotective because I always saw a certain amount of innocence in her. I could always see the dreams in her eyes. My mother had cancer, a quiet but meticulous thief.

Sadly enough, my Pops would literally carry my mom in his arms to the car, where he would place her for the dreadful ride to the hospital. This became a routine trip. I recall on this rainy day, the dark clouds that loomed over the neighborhood but even more in my heart as I watched my Pops take my mom to the hospital. The trees were whipping, and the winds sounded like a room full of baritones competing in a singing contest. He carefully lifted her, placing her fragile arms around his neck, as he swept her legs to a firm position. The rolling thunder sounded as though God was angry. In many ways, I empathized with those feelings because each time she had to leave, it left an empty place in my heart and fear I couldn't explain. He would put her in the car and drive away. The farther they drove, as I stood on my tippy-toes looking through the screened door, the rain folded behind the car like a curtain being lowered; soon, the car was no longer in sight. I spent the night with one eye opened hoping to hear my father and mother entering the door.

My two brothers slept in another room in proximity to mine. All I could think about was seeing my mom, contemplating about the many days I stood at the end of her bed looking at her, studying her face, and her mood. Some days, she appeared stoic and others I could see the tears rolling down her cheeks. Every once in a while, I could see a glimmer in the eyes as she marveled at us acting silly in the middle of the floor. Even then I could tell her dreams had not faded, but I felt a sense of transference of those dreams to me. One particular night, neither my Pops nor mom returned to the house late. Two days passed; three days passed. When my Pops came home, he looked tired and beaten up. I could see worry in his eyes. The next day in the late evening, when my Pops arrived, he loaded us in the car. As we drove, no one said anything. We drove into the parking lot of the hospital. It was dark, and at that time, the building looked so large. Walking into St. Dominic Hospital in Jackson, Mississippi, I remember seeing a plethora of women with black gowns looking almost penguin-like. When they walked, they moved around in groups, and they did it with their hands folded in front of their bodies; in fact, they didn't walk. They were gliding from one place to another, and they all looked mean. The hospital was cold too. We were taken into this waiting room where there was a statue of the Virgin Mary with her arms stretched out—unlike the penguins. It was scary and eerie to me as well. One at a time, they would take us to my mother's room. When it was my turn, I remember holding my Aunt Millie's hand walking; it seemed as though it took us forever to reach the room. When I entered, I saw a wall of people looking melancholic; I looked at the bed covered in white linens. My mom, "Mudear" as we called her, was lying under this plastic tent with her eyes barely opened. My Pops lifted me up to look at her, or so I thought, when in reality he lifted me for her to see me, as it would be the last time she would. My mom died moments later.

The next three days, I remember walking with my brothers behind my Pops who walked behind this gray casket. As we sat, I could hear people screaming; even then, it seemed surreal to me because I could not understand why. I saw when they opened the box and my mom laying there quietly. She had this blue gown on as she lay on her back with her eyes closed. I kept thinking, *These people are so darn loud, be quiet or you're going to wake my mom!* People were gathering in a line to look at her. I couldn't at that age wrap my mind around what was really going on. It wasn't until we went to the gravesite that a sense of finality came over me as they lowered this box with my mom in it into the ground. I had a feeling of separation, of distance, of the reality that I would never see her again, that she would not be returning home forever.

As for my father, I always thought he came from out of space. He was often quiet, but when he had something to say, everyone would listen. He was extremely observant, and that's why when he spoke, he was always on point. I could not totally understand my mom's attraction to him but felt it would be revealed more the older I got and the more I stayed around him. I did see the compassion and caring he gave my mom during her illness. He was a tall, dark, and handsome blue-black color—a true specimen of the motherland. He had the whitest teeth I had ever seen in my life—whiter than my mom's, and hers were bright. I always thought if you turned the light off at night and asked my Pops to open his mouth, we would be able to see! That was the inside joke I shared with my brothers Billy and Dobie whom were older than me.

My Pops wasn't an educated man. He was a brilliant carpenter and contractor by trade, and he was in demand for his work because he was good at what he did. White folks mostly had him working on their million-dollar homes. When my mom became ill, my father would have to take us with him on some of his jobs because we didn't have a babysitter. It was mostly me all the time that went with him because my brothers were involved in sports and they were never at home. He knew how to bullshit white folks when they talked about what they wanted. "Yes, sur," he would reply to them as they stood there acting with pleasure that they were superior just because they were white and he was a Negro. At nine years old, I could discern this because I was an active listener, but more than that, my Granny always told me about white folks and about them feeling privileged.

When my father would finish a job, to celebrate the beauty he produced, most white folks would invite him back to a party so they could introduce the miracle worker. I had on many occasions accompanied him to a party or two. As I stood there by his side hanging on to his suit coat, I watched how white folks talked to one another, each trying to one-up the next. I could hear how they bragged about their kids playing on football teams and how they were the star players. Mothers talked about their daughters being lead cheerleader for the varsity high school basketball or football teams. Most of the women were bottled blondes and never worked a day in their lives. Their greatest pride was how they raised their children. They were stay-at-home moms with privilege...white privilege. Their homes were pristine with spiral stairways that looked like they roped around for days. They had dark mahogany cabinets to match the dark mahogany floors. Long kitchen islands were with fruit stacked to the hilt. When I would leave my pop's side and wander about the house, I would walk out to the pool area where young white girls sat, laughed, and played with one another; they jumped into the prism of blue water, fading away as they swam to impress the skinny little white boys that stood by to watch them with their eyes cocked and their mouths hung open.

Yes, it was a site to see all right. The most interesting thing about the visits were the after-visits. I would go with my Pops after he left the fancy parties and dropped by Etta Mae's Bar & Soul Food Restaurant. He would meet his buddies there. I sat at the end of the bar drinking Coke while he talked to the rowdy group of men. Two heavy whiskies straight up on the rocks and he would start ripping, "Man, I just left them honkies. Man, them motherfuckers are crazy. I listen to them women talking while I'm working. Most of them are frustrated. Man, if I had offered them my dick, they would have jumped with a quickness." All the guys laughed, and they went back and forth talking about the horny women and white men with their tiny dicks. "Yeah, but them bastards pay me well though," my father quipped at the end of all the bantering.

At thirteen years old, I learned the real difference between blacks and whites. They integrated our schools in Jackson, and my Pops wanted me to go to the predominantly white school. He didn't necessarily want me to be with white folks, but he wanted me to be exposed to what they were getting: better books and all the offerings they didn't want black kids to have access to. Some black parents didn't share the wisdom of Pops. They believed separation was the best way to go; if we could receive the same books and access what white children had, there was no need to be with white folks, and they were not to be trusted. I agreed with their reasoning, but Pops was the boss. Granny once told me that any race of people that thought they discovered a country even though others were already in it could never be trusted. Why? Because they would always want what wasn't theirs and would be willing to get it by any means necessary. I always remembered that in my subliminal thoughts when dealing with Southern white folks.

So while Pops wanted me to be a part of the whole integration bit, he took a lot of flak for his decision to put us in integrated schools. Like most suppressed communities, or the poor blacks in Jackson, they were separated from the rich and upper-class folks by a railroad track. The railroad track was symbolic of the deeply rooted hatred and superiority mindset of white folks in the South. This served partly as the impetus for me to never accept failure.

We lived in a nice area because my Pops was the big shot carpenter and contractor. He was one of the first black contractors to own his own business. Our house was nice because my Pops did a lot of the work on it. So I guess you could call us middle-class black folks. He always wanted to be middle class but not too upper class because then he couldn't hang out with his buddies who were barely making ends meet, many of whom he hired to do jobs.

Mississippi had many dark histories. I remember in 1970, there was a shooting on the campus of Jackson State College, and in fact, two students were killed. This incident angered and hurt my father so deeply. I could hear his friends and him talking about the murders.

"They are the same motherfuckers that hire me to work for them daily, and I spend time perfecting their houses, the same ones who hate and hide as racists. And they call black folk niggers, you know?" my Pops lamented. "There is no excuse for shooting in a girl's dormitory, no excuse at all. I am so fucking mad," he said angrily. One college student and a high school student walking through the college campus had been shot and killed by the highway patrol. The racist governor had ordered them in to stop what they cited as rioting black students. When the story washed out, most blacks knew that wasn't true; most of us knew about how white boys were known for riding through the black college campus sexually harassing black college girls who would leave their dorms to cross the main street that separated the campus. The street was called Lynch Street. I always thought Lynch Street was named for what white folks were good at doing, lynching black people in the South, until Granny told me differently. Lynch Street was actually named for the first black Republican politician and speaker of the house in Jackson, Mississippi: John Lynch.

Anyway, this shooting stirred up something seriously. Supreme Court Justice Thurgood Marshall and other United States black congressmen visited Mississippi for an inquiry about college students shot during the massacre. Sad to say, years after the killing of the two students, it would be ruled justified. The irony was that Kent State University, an all-white college, one month earlier had gotten lots of attention for the shooting of white college students, yet black students received no attention at all in the press. For weeks my dad was frustrated and angry about that shooting. Most black folks who met at church on Sundays expressed disgust with the blatant racist act of violence and the racist governor who ordered the shooting as well. Good ole Mississippi, you either loved or hated it. Sometimes it was a combination of both. As for me, I maintained a state of duality about our great state; I loved it sometimes and hated others. When I was growing up, I hated it more than loving it.

There were other darkness I wanted to suppress myself because of shame and fear. I remember when I was ten years old, my Pops was trusting to leave me at his friend and distant family member named Johnny Ray. Johnny Ray had roaming hands. When I would finish eating and offered to wash dishes, he would double back into the kitchen when his wife went into the back. He'd come around and rub up against me as he passed the kitchen sink. It would make me sick. He once asked me to sit on his lap in front of his wife and friends. When I sat, I could feel the bulge of his private area get hard. It made me almost want to throw up. If I had to spend the night and sleep over in his daughter's room, I would have to sleep in the bottom bunk bed. There was no bargaining with his daughter Charmaine, as her favorite position was the top bunk. Around 1:30 a.m., when it was pitch dark in the room, Johnny Ray would slip into the room stealthily, pull down the covers, and put his hands into my panties touching my private area. I would move his hand and start crying. He'd put his finger to his lip to gesture to me to stop crying. The next morning, he would always say it was our little secret. This went on for years, and I was afraid to tell my Pops because I knew he would kill Johnny Ray and then I wouldn't have a Pops. It was a frightening thought that he would have to go to Parchment, the prison of choice in Mississippi. To avoid staying over Johnny Ray's, I begged my Pops to take me with him during summer months; I told him I could read a book while he worked. "Pops, please?" I would say, "I promise I won't say a word." Finally, he took a chance and consented.

Meeting of the Minds

IN THE SUMMER of 1970, I was thirteen years old. Not long after the massacre at Jackson State College, Pops worked on a huge job for the lieutenant governor of Mississippi. He spent many hours working that job. I sat out by the pool in the shade each day, reading. One day, this teenage white boy who looked around sixteen years old came by the pool. He was a little different from most white boys I saw down in Mississippi. He was cute; he had jet-black hair, a little longer than how most white boys in Mississippi would wear theirs. He had olive-colored skin, darker than most boys from the Sip too. Above all, he was friendly. "Hey," he said, and I wasn't sure he was talking to me. I ignored him and kept reading. It was great because I had these extremely dark glasses on and pela pusher pants with a short top. I had my hair in a long ponytail. I ignored him and did not respond. He jumped in the water and swam several laps in the pool. When he swam to the entrance of the pool, this time he came out of it. I lifted my head up to watch the water cascade down his body on to his rippled muscles. I quickly pulled myself together because I'd never had the thoughts I felt about any male, let alone a white boy. I was thirteen but could easily be mistaken for a seventeen-year-old. I was tall and mature-looking. My eyes turned back into my novel *The*

Spook Who Sat by the Door by Sam Greenlee. When I looked at his body, I saw my life flash in front of me, perpetuated by the thought of my Pops hanging me if he even had an inkling I was thinking about a white boy.

He walked over to me and struck up a conversation. "Hi," he said, "I'm George. My uncle is the lieutenant governor. I spend summers with him. I'm from Chicago. Who are you?"

I looked up and said, "Hi, my name is Lisa." I extended my hand out to shake his as my grandmother always taught me. "My Pops is contracted to work for your uncle."

He told me he was seventeen years old. He shared with me what he liked about school in Chicago and what he didn't like. I discovered we had a lot in common. The only obvious thing was he was white and I was black. I sat and listened attentively, and my amygdala was working in overtime. I shared with him what I liked about school. I found out we had a definite shared passion for music—jazz. He knew many of the jazz musicians I spoke of and I his. Time passed fast, and soon my Pops was waving for me to go. I said goodbye to George and stuck my hand out to seal the departure.

Since it was the weekend, I had all weekend to ruminate about the conversation I had with someone decent from another race. At our school, white kids were usually curiously nasty or walked around with a superior attitude. I wasn't especially liked because they looked at me as an uppity nigger. You know, the kinda black person that was smart and wasn't taking any shit from them. The kinda girl that would check them if they said something out of order. I always thought about what my Granny said to me, "LiLi, you have to beat white folks with what they are most afraid of, you being smart and intelligent." I took her at her word and used that as my weapon of choice against the racist, condescending white girls and boys who often wanted to say something out of whack but wouldn't to me. My height, intelligence, and color of skin threatened them the most. The white kids that spent time away during the summer were usually friendly. I surmised it was because they had been exposed to more black people.

Over the weekends, I would go to the country or rural area to visit my Granny. She was a total mess! I loved my Granny because she was always on one hundred. She was my paternal Granny. I could see where my Pops got his craziness. Granny had this big ole house in Chrystal Springs, Mississippi. She lived alone after years of living with my paw paw that died; he was a farmer. My granddad's farm used to have lots of food. My brothers and I would run down rows of cucumbers, tomatoes, cabbage, and okra. You name it, he had it. On days when we were tired from running, we would stop and grab a tomato and eat it right on the spot. We enjoyed getting the old Black Phantom bikes and riding up and down the hills. There was no other feeling of freedom when I visited my Granny. The most important time for me was the one-on-one time I had with my Granny. We called it girl time. We would get in the old, banged-up red vintage Ford truck two-seater. She would throw the picnic basket in the back with a jug of iced lemonade in a box. My Granny was beautiful. She was of medium height and had caramel complexion. She had the most beautiful head of gray hair; she looked like a silver fox. She wore this old straw hat on her head sometimes. As she was driving to our special place, she would hum this old song "Hold On." I didn't say a word; I just listened, savoring the time I had with her. Looking out of the window, we would pass old farms that were no longer farms but were still standing and dirt roads where people would travel to and from to get to their loved ones. I saw people sitting on porches, happy people laughing, and I imagined telling jokes that only they could relate to.

We would drive off the road through green trees, branches sticking out and hitting the top of the truck as we made our way through to our own spot. As we got closer, I could see the smile on my Granny's face. A sudden stop, and "Well, we're here, sweetie." Every time I stepped out of the truck, it was always like it was my first time. I would close my eyes and feel the breeze that sometimes felt as though it was lifting me to new heights. When I opened my eyes, there it was, this tall tree with its limbs spread out so far you couldn't distinguish the tree from the greenery on the ground. It was so large, but it could not match the magnitude of the moment.

Granny signaled to me to get the lemonade out the back of the truck. I ran happily around the truck to retrieve it. She pulled a quilt she had made just for us and a blanket from the truck as well. We took both sides of the picnic basket and found our spot. Granny took one end of the blanket and I the other and whooshed it into the air. It landed on the ground right beneath the sycamore tree. Birds were chirping, crickets were sounding off, and every now and then the sun would peak through the large leaves that were stretched out far across the pond. You could hear the sound of the water as it made its way downstream to other destinations unknown. She laid the picnic basket carefully down and I the jug of lemonade. Granny pulled off her shoes and took off her hat. She opened the basket with the sandwiches she had made; she also had pickled cucumbers, salted peanuts, corn on the cob, and her delicious German chocolate cake. She gave me a towel and a small pillow covered with the knitting pillowcase she had made.

The first ten minutes would be moments of solitude. Granny always said sometimes we have to stop and listen to nature. She said when you do that, you will find answers, you will find peace, and you will find yourself. She would lean against the huge trunk of the tree, and I'd put my head in her lap with eyes closed pointed toward the sky but my ears sharp. We said nothing. After fifteen minutes or so, Granny would ask me what's going on with me. I would usually tell her about what had happened during the school year and would have her laughing at the craziness I experienced with white kids. She would laugh so hard but sanctioned what I said and did. I shared with Granny that I had met this one white boy at the lieutenant governor's house. I told her about the conversation we had. She said to me friends have no color. Friendship comes from the heart; the only toughest part of friendship is it has to be earned. "It's an invaluable commodity," Granny would say. "You have to earn friendship because once you earn something, you take care of it. You don't damage or hurt it, you take care of it. You understand?" I nodded my head. "Friendship is a close friend of trust. They work hand and hand. A person has to earn trust too," she said. "Neither one is an automatic given, LiLi. With trust and friendship comes respect. You will have to determine how you mitigate that, my child."

I smiled at Granny and then said, "Can we eat now?"

She laughed, and we ate.

Chapter 3

Living Out Dreams

THE WEEKEND WENT by so fast. It was time to get back to Jackson. On the ride back, I asked Pops how much longer would he be working on the lieutenant governor's house. He said he would probably finish it by the end of the summer. In my head, I was thinking, *Okay, so you have a few more weeks to learn more about George;* but I would never say that to my Pops or anyone else for that matter.

On that Monday when we arrived at the house, I sat in the truck for about ten minutes to listen to music on the truck radio. I would listen to Grover Washington, one of my favorite instrumental jazz musicians. When I finally decided to go into the house, the family was eating breakfast together. I spoke, "Good morning," and kept going out near the pool area with my novel in hand. I sat by the pool, and my Pops came and sat by me. He was waiting for one of his workers to bring a tool to him, so he had time to chat. "What you reading?" he asked.

"I'm reading Sam Greenlee's *The Spook Who Sat by the Door*," I said.

"Oh yeah, that's a good book. Did you know Sam Greenlee is from Chicago?"

While I had read that he was, I really didn't make a connection that George was from the same place.

Pops said, "He's really controversial. The real CIA was on his ass for writing this book."

Wow, I didn't know that, but most of all, I was shocked my Pops knew it. He could really surprise me sometimes. He asked me to tell him what I thought about the book. At that time, his worker showed up with the tool, and they both went back to work.

Twenty minutes later, George came out for a morning swim. I kept reading and never looked up, not even to speak again. When he finished his laps, he walked toward me, drying off. "Hey there."

I looked up and said, "Hi."

"Still reading the same book?"

"Yep. The author of this book is from Chicago, Sam Greenlee."

"Oh, really? Never heard of him."

I said, "Maybe you should read the novel."

"Maybe I should," he said.

He shared with me that he was going to tour the University of Mississippi as he was thinking about going to law school there. I told him that was great. "Why law?" I asked. He said it was somewhat of a family legacy. He explained his dad and uncles all were lawyers. I asked, "Is that what you really want to do, be a lawyer?" He asked why was I curious. Well, I told him my Granny always said it is always best to do something your heart is invested in. "Is your heart invested in being a lawyer? George admitted his heart was not. But he felt his parents would not accept anything else. He really wanted to be a master chef and travel to Paris. "Then do it!" I shouted. He smiled at me. He wondered what I wanted to become, and I told him I wanted to become a fashion magazine editor and I am going to Paris one day. We talked about it, and I had to remind him he'd better get going. As he walked away, I smiled, and he turned and smiled as well.

The following week was the last week of summer and the last week my Pops would be working on that contract. That Friday, my Pops was invited to come to the finish party at the house he had worked on. I dressed for the party this time with due diligence. I put my hair in a ponytail slicked back; I had a white off-the-shoulder cotton dress with sandals. When we arrived at the party, there were a lot of people and a lot of kids as well. I walked in with Pops and scanned the room. Politicians were talking politics, and politicians' wives were salivating over the changes the lieutenant governor's wife had made. She was queen for a day.

Most of the young people were out by the pool. I looked way across the pool and spotted George. Absolutely no one said anything to me. In fact, they were looking as though I was lost or I was the help. I sat down near the pool in my regular chair and crossed my legs with my shades on. I sat and observed how the girls and boys reacted and responded to George. As soon as he saw me, he made a B line right over to where I was sitting. I reached my hand out again and said hello. He sat at the end of the pool chair and started chatting. If I could have bottled the looks of both the guys and girls that very moment, it would have been a perfect gift for my Granny. We talked awhile, and later that night, when he went into the house, I walked to my pop's car to listen to jazz. Miles Davis's "Kind of Blue" was playing. I laid on the hood of the car, listening to Miles. George came out and laid beside me. "Miles?" he said.

"Yes, it is, and I love it," I quipped.

We lay there quietly respecting the music, and we both agreed that he had created his most indisputable masterpiece. "Do you believe in dreams?" he asked me.

"Yes, I do. I always saw dreams in my mom's eyes. I now have them in mine."

"So do I." He took out a pencil and gave me his phone number and address. "I hope to hear from you."

I looked at him and said, "I hope so too."

Months would follow and George and I would write to each other. Sometimes I would write a letter during a boring science lab. I would drop the letter in the mailbox that stood right outside the school. Once a week, I would check our mailbox, anticipating a letter from him. This went on for two years, and the letters stopped. I tried calling, but the number was disconnected. It was a complete puzzle.

I went into my drawer to read the last letter I got from George for clues:

> Dear Lisa:
>
> It was great to hear from you. It's been pretty hectic for me, you know, trying to handle law school and all. As you know, I decided to go to a law school here in Chicago, the University of Chicago, because mom thought it was better than the University of Mississippi. Even though my uncles attended UM, she was fine that I decided to stay in Chicago.
>
> You were right, Lisa, it is important to follow your passion. I always remembered your question: "Are you invested into being a lawyer?" I've finally answered that question.
>
> Take care until we meet again.
>
> George

This was the last letter I received from him. I didn't have a clue as to how he had reconciled becoming a lawyer. All I know is I had a great disconnect to a friend. It left me wondering and somewhat empty to boot. Until we meet again? I always wondered when, as the years passed so fast.

Becoming an Adult

I RECEIVED A scholarship to attend Parsons School of Design in New York. It was a definite coup. In 1975, there were only three blacks graduating from Central High School, and I was one of them. I was so excited to have the opportunity to go to one of the best fashion institutions and, most importantly, to get away and lose the past of the sexual abuse delivered by my pop's distance cousin and best friend. I needed change. I was very surprised that my Pops was willing to let me go so far away. He planned a weekend for us in New York so he could help me find an apartment in Greenwich Village. Talking with my Pops, I discovered he felt I was very mature. It made me feel so confident! "Thanks, pop," I said after our big talk.

The weekend before I was scheduled to leave with Pops, I visited Granny. When I came through the door, I ran into her arms. She held me so tight. "Look at you, getting ready to make us proud." I knew that this day was going to be special, and she did as well. She spent some time with Pops, talking with him. I was so anxious to go on our picnic. We went through the same routine. The journey to our private spot this time would be poignant. Granny fixed a special picnic lunch this time for me, including chicken sandwiches, pickles, cookies, muffins, and a Coke. Our solitude moment meant much to me because Granny would rub my head and hum her favorite song again: "Hold On." She imparted lots of wisdom to me. I could feel she had confidence in me, but she wanted to ensure I knew I had confidence. When we drove away, I looked at my Granny as she waved to me with tears in my eyes.

I was floored to discover my Pops had planned the trip to New York without a hitch. This man still amazed me. He had a friend in New York, Tom Wildford, whom he had worked with before. Tom lived in Harlem. He was a well-known contractor and had worked on Earl Graves's (owner of Black Enterprise) brownstone in Harlem with Pop's help. Tom knew the ropes and had basically done all the footwork for us. He had found the apartment. The rent was sent to him to make the downpayment plus rent for two months. We were scheduled to fly out that weekend, two weeks before I was due to start school.

We flew to New York. My eyes were as large as fifty-cent pieces as I looked out of the plane window at the skyline. My heart skipped several beats. This was all new to me. I was about to start my adult life and to find out about myself—something that my Granny always sanctioned. We hopped into a taxi to Greenwich Village to meet Tom. Along the way, I got a crash course in city life. The streets were crowded even at night. People moved fast and talked even faster. The taxi driver never stopped talking. Pops would look over at me and roll his eyes. I was wondering how much more of it he could take before going one hundred on the driver. We pulled up to 243 Bleecker Street #4438. At first glance, I thought, *What? This is a pastry shop!*

When we got out of the taxi, Tom called out, "Jack! Hey, man!" They shook each other's hands and man-hugged. "Well, welcome to New York, young lady!"

"Tom, this is Lisa. Lisa, this is Tom," Pops said.

"Hi," I replied.

He started talking about the area; supposedly it was a trendy area, high density, and hip people lived in the area.

The apartment was above the pastry shop with a separate entrance. The apartment was ideal. It was a two-bedroom with hardwood floors. There were windows in every room and hardwood and ceramic tile flooring throughout the apartment. Pop's friend had found a winner. Once we sat the suitcases down, Tom invited us out to dine at a local restaurant. We went to this quaint restaurant called the Tandoor not too far from the apartment. It was an ethnic restaurant filled with people from all cultures. It was almost like sitting in the United Nations. He wanted to quickly know what had been going on with my Pops. "Hey, how is our friend doing, Johnny Ray?" he asked. I nearly fell out of my chair when he asked about Johnny Ray. Tom was laughing as he talked about some of the craziness Johnny Ray had exhibited while he was visiting Jackson. As fate would have it, Johnny Ray had developed cancer of the colon and was not able to get around like he used to. I thought, *Reciprocity is a bitch, isn't it?*

We returned to the apartment after thanking Tom, and he wished me the best. He gave me a card and assured me I could call him anytime I needed help. Since the apartment was furnished, it made it easier to put away my things. Pops slept in one of the rooms, and I, of course, had the big room. The first week with him was spent learning the city and how to ride the subway trains and buses. We went to the grocery store, but I also learned about the bodegas. They were what we called convenience stores in the neighborhood. New York City's bodegas proved to be more than just delis; they're coffee shops, community centers, watering holes, snack bars, and places to gossip or gather information. It's also where you go to get your morning egg and cheese, buy beer, satisfy that midnight snack craving, and meet your neighbors to boot.

On the day my Pops left, I was sad. He had the talk with me about being careful, getting in before dark if I could, watching my back, and most of all not trusting anyone. He hopped into a taxi from the apartment to the airport. When he left, I bounced on the bed and laid on my back, looking at the ceiling fan. I was about to start my life.

Friends in High Places

STARTING MY LIFE at Parsons was everything I had hoped it to be. Not many of us—meaning, black folks—were there. The classes were challenging, but because I wanted it so badly, I didn't mind.

I met this crazy and wild New Yorker named Amanda. She was a very loud black girl, the total opposite of me, but she was so friendly, and people in the class liked her a lot. She always sat two rows down from me. After a class one night, she invited us to join her at one of the local clubs called the Village Vanguard. I didn't really know what type of club it was, but what the hell, I wanted to find out. The club was in Greenwich at seventh and Greenwich lane, which was sweet because I lived in the village. We hopped taxies to the club. Looking at the place from the outside, you would never know it existed. But once you got in it, it was like heaven. It was a speakeasy jazz club. I would have *never* figured Amanda to be someone who liked jazz. Just goes to show you can't judge a book by the cover. I was so pumped. I really wasn't at the appropriate age to drink, and I honored that; but because I was tall and lanky, I kinda fell in with the others that were at the right age. I just wanted to hear good jazz.

Amanda was really cool. She was two years ahead of me and had two more years to go. Like me, she was a tall dark-skinned girl with long legs and arms. She wore this huge Afro with a cropped top. She had on bell-bottom pants with platform sandals. She had these really big hoops on her ears. Most of the girls dressed like that, and I thought it was so cool. Me, I had on a really short summer cotton dress with platform sandals. My old, faithful ponytail was now put up in a ponytail bun. The two guys—correction, gals—that were with us had tall Afros as well, but they had tight bell bottoms that floored widely over their shoes. They, too, had cropped tops on. Donnie and Greg both adored Amanda. I looked around the club like a kid in a candy store. So much history there. The pictures on the wall featured so many famous jazz greats that had performed in the club. I kept thinking, *Wow, George would get lost in this place like me.*

The club played jazz music until the live music started. Max Roach was a regular there, and he was beyond my expectations. We sat and talked about our professors; Greg had a crush on one of them. He was killing us, smacking his lips, and sipping on a drink. The liquor was getting to him fast because he started talking about if he married the professor. The more he talked and snapped his fingers talking shit, the more we were all dying. Amanda was puffing him up too to get more shit talking out of him as well. Amanda said her brother would be joining us as soon as he left his job.

"You have a brother, huh?"

"Yea, he's my big brother and my only brother. It's just two of us. I'm the baby girl, you can say. He's interning at a company uptown, and he'll join us soon," she said.

We had that in common. "I have two brothers, and they are older than me. Both have started their careers. Billy owns a local radio station in Mississippi, and Dobie is a dentist there as well," I shared.

The lights blinked, and the stage lights went up, and the house-lights went dark. The main musicians came on stage and started jamming. Later, the house emcee came up and introduced the vocalist for that night. "And now, ladies and gentlemen, help me welcome to the stage, Ms. Carmen McCrae." The intimate crowd clapped loudly, and I just about pissed my pants. Carmen McCrae, oh shit. I done died and gone to heaven. Ms. McCrae came out on stage, and the first song she belted out was "Round Midnight." Three minutes into the song, this tall dark-skinned, bearded hunk of a specimen walked up to the table. He hugged Amanda and sat down. He was dressed in a dark suit with a white shirt and tie. He sat down and locked right into McCrae immediately. Carmen had mesmerized everyone in the room. I had never experienced anything like that night. When she wrapped up the set, Amanda introduced us to her brother. Of course, the gals had to overdo it. They were batting eyes and talking proper as well. Amanda started kidding her brother about wearing a suit. He played it off and laughed back at her. We decided to go grab something to eat.

One of the biggest adjustments I had to make when I moved to New York was how late they liked to stay out partying. Going out to get food at twelve midnight would be a fleeting thought if I were in Mississippi. It was a big adjustment. Anyway, we found this perfect little spot with the best corned-beef sandwiches and fries. I got a chance to talk with Amanda's brother. "Hi, I'm Lisa," I said. I reached my hand out to shake his, and he obliged me.

He replied, "Oh, hi, I'm Malik." He asked if I was a student, and of course, I told him all about my classes. Malik was a smart guy with great ambitions. He wanted to become the richest architect in New York, not just the richest African American architect. He was very invested into what he was doing. I was certainly charmed by Malik. He really had a good head on his body and a slamming body to match.

Two days after this unforgettable night, I saw Amanda in class. After we walked out, she caught up with me. "Girl, where you been?"

I said, "Oh, just trying to get some storyboards done. It's been really crazy with the turnaround time on the syllabus."

"Yeah, I know. I remember that class, and the teacher is an ass-hole, but he is good. You won't regret the work you do," she added.

We walked to a neighborhood coffee shop. "What's going on with you?" I asked.

"Oh, girl, I only have a few more classes, and I'm out. I can't wait," she said. Amanda was so smart and creative. She wanted to leave New York and live in Milan. Her parents had high expectations for their kids, and Amanda had high expectations for herself as well. She showed me her portfolio she was working on. I was astonished at how dynamic it was. "Oh yes, my brother was very smitten with you. He asked if he could get your phone number so you guys could hook up some time."

"Sure," I said.

"Okay, I'll give it to him. Just a warning, he is very charming, so watch yourself."

As she walked away, I thought, *Hm...consider your warning taken seriously, sister,* although I didn't know what to expect.

A week had passed, and I hadn't seen Amanda; I thought it was because she was preparing her portfolio. I had been in class all day long, and I was so tired. When I entered my apartment, I flopped on the bed giving view to the ceiling fan. I'd had many nights when the ceiling fan was my focal for sleep. Sometimes I would awake the next day with my clothes on. It was the panacea for good sleep. When it would rain and the ceiling fan was going, gosh, I was in sleep heaven. There was something about the rain that calmed my spirit. It seemed I was more aware of the purposefulness of my body and its natural existence. It reminded me of the conversations I used to have with Granny about death and the fact that we turn into ashes. Granny used to say you go back to what you were made of, earth. So I always made that connection to rain and sleep—an exquisite partnership for solitude and peace while on earth.

Time passed so fast because before I could catch a breath. We had already gone through one and a half years in my time at Parsons. Each of us was operating on all cylinders. I had projects galore, and so did Greg, Donnie, and Amanda. Greg took a few months off from school because he was ill with sickle cell. We would meet often to keep in good spirit. Also, we all took turns to check in on him, cook meals, and encourage him, willing him back to good health.

In June 1977, I was home lying down after a long day. Twenty minutes into my comatose, the phone rang. I literally crawled over to the phone. "Hello," I said.

"Hey, you, this is Malik. I thought I'd call to invite you to mine and Amanda's party our parents are giving us. You know, she graduates, and I finish my internship."

"Oh, hi, Malik. Thanks for the invitation. When is it?"

"It's Saturday at seven p.m. Meet us at the Century Association, at Forty-Third Street between Fifth and Sixth Avenues, okay?"

"Okay, what's the attire?" I said.

"It's the best, baby!" he quickly said.

I had three days to get my shit together. I called the two gals, Donnie and Greg. I thought this would be a great opportunity to get Greg out of his apartment. In addition, they loved it, as it gave them a chance to show off their fashion prowess. I met them on Friday at Saks Fifth Avenue. They were dressed for the occasion. Greg came in full regalia—a red-colored boa, red-and-white shirt with buttons all the way to the neck, and bell-bottom blue jeans. Donnie always just kept it simple: a pair of jeans and a white shirt. They pranced around selecting items until they had quite the stack of things for me to try on. As I went in to try on dresses, they would consult with each other and give me a thumbs up or a thumbs down. The salesladies loved them; they brought them champagne, and they were feeling it too. Finally, when I came out with this long fitted black-and-white maxi dress made of chiffon, they cut up. "Yes, baby, you better give it to me!" Fingers were snapping all over the place. I couldn't help myself. I was in tears laughing. When we left the store, they walked me over to another street in Manhattan to a costume jewelry store. There they accessorized me. To thank them for their help, I treated them to lunch. Without a doubt, it was an experience.

Dicknified

I WENT HOME after lunch with Greg and Donnie and dropped on the bed, tired from watching them shop and from the big lunch I had. I slept for two hours. Around 6:00 p.m., I started the ritual for getting dressed. I took a long-soaked bath and listened to the music oozing from my record player. Coltrane was the music of choice. I thought about my brothers who always told me I had an old soul, even older than theirs; after all, they were older than me. I loved jazz. I had no problem hanging around older folks, and most of my friends were older as well. So I accepted that I had an old soul. As I lay in the bubbled bathtub, the phone rang, and of course, I had to run for the phone in the bedroom. "Hello," I answered.

It was Malik. "Hey, you, just checking to make sure you're coming tonight."

I told him I was in the process of preparing to come. He said he'd hang up then because he knew, when his sister said that, it meant an hour or two preparations. I started getting dressed, and the phone rang again, and wouldn't you know it, it was the gals checking to see if I needed any help. I told them I was okay and told them I would see them there.

I waved a taxi to the club and started thinking what to anticipate. I couldn't imagine because Amanda was almost an enigma. Just when I thought I got her, she would show me something totally different. She was very different from her brother Malik. He was kinda in-your-face "I'm all that and I know it." I loved his confidence because it was edgy to cockiness. That didn't bother me because my brothers were like Malik, very confident and self-assured. When I arrived, the taxi door came open, and the doorman welcomed us to the Century Association. He took my hand, and I lifted out of the taxi. The club was a palazzo-style building. Walking through the club, it seemed very majestic. The hallways were graced with eloquent carpet and wide too. The walls were dark wood from wall to wall. I passed rooms with huge bookshelves from floor to ceiling. The chandeliers were stunning in each room. The gentleman led me through this banquet-like room draped in beautiful black-and-white tablecloths until finally we came to the door of the terrace. It was crowded with older men and women in tuxedos and women with long dresses. It was a diverse group of people of all races, cultures, and ages.

When I walked around to find either Malik or Amanda, I could tell I was in the presence of success. I looked across the room and saw Amanda. I waved to her, and she came over immediately. "Hey, girl, glad you made it." She was being Amanda, but not as loud as she usually would be. "Have you seen Malik yet?" she asked.

"No, not yet," I replied.

Then two gentlemen walked up to me in tuxedos, tall, dark, and proper. And let me tell you, I almost spit the water out of my mouth. What the fuck! It was Donnie and Greg dressed like men. When I saw them and before I could open my mouth, Greg stopped me, whispering to me, "Bitch, don't go there." I had tears flowing from my eyes. Once I got my shit together, I told them how nice they looked. Amanda whispered in my ear, "Honey, they knew my Pops wouldn't have that bullshit dressing." It seemed they knew how to adapt for this crowd.

Someone signaled it was time to go into the banquet area. So we transitioned from cocktails (in my case, water) to the banquet.

Name cards were on every table. Amanda grabbed my hand; and Greg, Donnie, and I followed her to our table. Malik was already there. The gentleman he was, he stood up until Amanda and I sat down. The old queens followed. "Hey, you," Mailk said.

"Hi, congratulations to both of you for your accomplishments!"

They thanked me, and the banquet was in progress. To watch the servers was like watching a ballet. They were eloquent, polite, and proficient. They served the tables quickly. I was thinking the food and ambience were tits. Malik was seated next to me. We talked awhile about him wrapping up his internship. Malik was really good at his career; I learned he had been given the lead on some major projects in New York. I was impressed, and so was he. He had been offered a job already, courtesy of his firm and his dad as well, with an architecture firm in New York. "Wow, you move fast, don't you?" I quipped.

He smiled and said, "That's the way it is if you want to meet the goals I have." I nodded my head and smiled.

One of the stray old ladies that was seated at our table engaged Amanda. Amanda told her she was leaving in a month to go to Milan, Italy. "I'm so proud of you two. Although, Amanda, I know your mom and dad wanted you to choose another profession, I'm glad you stuck with your gut. Good for you!"

Oh, I said to myself, "Mom and dad kind of bossy."

His father came to the microphone on the dais and welcomed everyone for coming to celebrate his children. He announced Malik's start at the architecture firm and Amanda's departure to Milan in a month. The audience applauded. He called them both to the dais, and they went. Amanda was reluctant but with a smile. Being the gentleman he is, Malik motioned to his sister to speak first. I have to tell ya, Amanda once again surprised me, and she spoke so eloquently thanking her parents, family, and friends for their support of her. Malik, on the other hand, did the same but went further to say what his intent was. "Thanks to my dad and mom. They have always entertained my telling them I was headed for success. Thanks to my colleagues from the firm. I never thought of anything else because I knew what I wanted to do. Not just do it but to do it successfully. I thank them for encouraging me and being there for me to help me work through my arrogance and helping humble myself in the process. Thanks, Mom and Dad." He got applause from the people and especially his parents.

When they returned to the table, I congratulated them again. There was a dance floor, so after the accolades were given, the music started, and people went on the floor to dance. Malik asked me to go with him. In the banquet room, there was an area at the top of the stairs on both sides where you could stand and look over at guests. I went with him. Not one to mince his words, he immediately asked me if I knew why he asked me to come, and I said, "Besides the obvious?"

He said, "Yes, of course."

I said no. He began to tell me how he was intrigued with me and wanted to get to know me more. I said, "Okay, let's do that. Let's get to know each other." He reached for my hand, and it felt great. I thought, *Well, here we go,* me taking a quantum leap into being a woman.

Chapter 7

Swimming in Deep Waters

AT THE END of the night, when people were saying their good-byes, Amanda invited me to go with them to a dance club; and before I could say yes, Malik said, "No, I've already invited her to go with me. I'm meeting some friends from the firm."

I looked at him and said, "Okay, I'm going with Malik, and I'll catch up with you guys later."

Malik introduced me to his parents at the end as a friend of Amanda's that went to Parsons. They were polite and nice. I extended my hand to them and shook both hands. His dad cited, "I like that handshake." I smiled. Right after that, we left in a taxi and met Malik's friends at an apartment in Manhattan. They were mostly white boys with girlfriends and maybe two other black guys. The two black guys were nice. Their girlfriends were white, and they had been interns at the firm as well. I surmised this was his circle of friends, and he didn't seem to mind at all. When he introduced me, they were nice and cordial, but I could tell I was swimming in a sea of confidence from all of them, almost a narcissistic pool of slush. They had cocktails, and I was asked what I wanted. They were surprised to hear me say "Pellegrino." I didn't drink.

We sat on a couch and talked awhile, and Malik asked about me. I started telling him that which I had not already offered to share. He leaned over and kissed me on my lips. It was nice. It was my first kiss, and it was a new feeling. By then I was eighteen years old and still a virgin. I intended to stay one until that special person came along. That was the commitment I made to myself. We would talk more, and he would kiss my lips more. I excused myself to go to the bathroom. I closed the door behind me and placed my back against the door. I said to myself, "Self, this is nice, but I need to tell him this is as far as it goes. After all, he is much older than me."

When I came out, he was standing at the bar, getting a drink, and talking with a friend. He would glance every once in a while over and smile at me. I got a chance to know some others in the room. I had a conversation with Carol, a white girl that had interned with Malik. She was nice but nosey. She was so curious about me and how I met Malik. I would turn the questions back to her and found out that's how she stopped being nosey.

Around 2:00 a.m., I was ready to depart. I told Malik I was ready. He said, "Already?"

I told him, "Yes, it's been a long day."

He said goodbye to his friends, and we grabbed a taxi. In the taxi, he asked me what I thought about his friends. I was honest; they were nice, and I said to him they all spoke alike. He laughed and said that was the voices of success. When we pulled up at my place, I told him thank you and I enjoyed myself. He looked a little surprised I didn't invite him in. Not. I told him I would talk with him next week. He gave me a kiss on the lips and said good night. The taxi didn't pull away until I was in my apartment.

The next month or so, I went out on a few dates with Malik after that night, and he was always very kind. I knew, however, one of those dates would lead to him wanting to be closer to me more than I was ready to be. He had a roommate who interned with him. I went over to his place one night after we had gone to the Broadway show *Bubbling Brown Sugar*. His place was a typical shared male apartment. I sat down at the table across from him. He fixed himself a drink and asked if I wanted one. The answer was always no—just was not a drinker. He came over and stood over me. He said, "I want to make love to you."

I looked at him and said, "I'm not ready." I told him that was a serious decision to be made and one with the person some day I would be with forever.

He stepped back and looked at me. "Are you serious?"

I said "As a matter of fact, yeah."

"Well," he said, "I'm a little taken back. I thought we were pretty tight."

I had to explain to Malik we were getting to know each other, and there were so many things I didn't know about him.

I told him I knew he was ambitious and wanted to be the best architect ever, but beyond the two months we had been dating, I needed to know more to trust him. After that, he seemed okay, but I thought I'd just jump into a taxi and leave. He hailed a taxi for me, kissed me on the forehead, and I left. When I got to my place, I thought about that evening. I had no regrets. I liked Malik, but I was not in love with Malik.

A week went past, and I was really bogged down knee-deep in projects I had to complete before the end of the semester. On that Monday night, Amanda called and asked me to meet her at this swank little pub where most of the Parsons students would hangout. I met her there around 7:00 p.m. She was so happy because in one more week, she'd be off to Milan on her life journey. We sat and talked, and then Donnie and Greg dropped in. We laughed at shit we did that was so whacked. While Greg and Donnie had one more semester, I started to feel I was losing my friends to life. Amanda mentioned she had asked Malik to drop off something she needed to take with her to Milan, but he had been so busy he didn't drop it off. She suggested that on our way home, we would drop in on him; she had a key. We walked for several blocks, and finally we were at Mailk's crib. We went up, she opened the door, and we went in. We heard noises, and when she called out, no one answered. Then Greg, the messy queen he was, said, "Let's go see." And we did, we opened the door, and there you had it, ass to the world. All I could see was Malik standing by the bed and this girl with his dick in her mouth. We were stunned, but not as much as him. We all ran back into the living room with our eyes cocked and mouths opened. We said nothing.

Malik was so angry with Amanda, and they had a few words. "Hey, man, don't get angry with me. I been calling your black ass and asking you to bring my stuff and you been working. I called out, and nobody answered, so you literally got caught with your drawers down." We stepped outside the apartment and waited for Amanda. Donnie and Greg were on a roll with their comments. I just laughed. None of them knew I had gone on several dates with Malik, but I did; that's what mattered. When Amanda came down, we all folded over laughing. Amanda said, "What the fuck did he expect?" We walked our ways, and I decided to hop a taxi home. As I'm sitting in the taxi, I remembered the girl who was hanging on his dick; it was Carol. She was the girl that sat and talked with me and was quite nosey, I must say, the night I went to the party with Malik. Now it was clear to me; she loved Malik, and I guess I have to say, they obviously were in some type of relationship. Later on, Amanda told me Carol was the daughter of the senior partner at the architecture firm where Malik was tracking. I really did see where Malik was going with it. Everything was about business for Malik; he was positioning himself quite well, no pun intended! I patted myself on the back and said, "Bravo, baby, bravo!" I was so glad I did not sleep with him. A couple of days would go by, and he left a few messages on the answering machine. I hadn't responded because I was so swamped in work.

On that Friday, when I was at home, I returned the calls; and he didn't pick up, so I left a message. "Malik, hey, I'm sorry we invaded your privacy. I found no joy in doing that. I want you to know I am happy for you. I get it, and I want you to be as successful as you say you are going to be. You're still my friend, and I'll call you soon or see you when I meet Amanda, Greg, and Donnie for her going-away rendezvous. Take care, Malik." I hung up the phone, and I felt nothing.

Chapter 8

Letters from the Heart

AMANDA LEFT FOR Milan the end of August 1977. I, on the other hand, kept myself busy the remainder of the summer. I took a week off the last week of July before the next semester and went home to visit Pops. When I flew into the airport, I looked out the window. There was no skyline, just the beautiful greenery you only got to see in Central Park while jogging. We flew over the Jackson reservoir, and it was a beautiful site to see. My Pops was waiting at the gate. "Hey, Pops!" He gave me a hug, and we went headed out of the terminal to the car.

"Where is your luggage?" he would ask.

"Well, Pops, since I am only here for a week, I packed lightly. I had a carry-on."

It was so nice to be at home and wake up in my own bed. You could hear the birds chirping and people's lawns being mowed early in the morning. I could smell the coffee in the kitchen. Pops had hired a cleaning service for himself because he didn't have the time. They were busy cleaning the house.

The next day, I cooked dinner and invited my brothers and their wives over. It was nothing like family being together, old jokes, old pictures being shared, updates on what was going on in Jackson.

My Pops had plenty to share, plenty. He was privy to another side of white folks. He knew when they were having affairs, both the men and women. He knew when they would have private meetings, and he knew when their kids were sneaking and drinking and experimenting with drugs when the parents were not around. He had some good ones to talk about. My brothers, on the other hand, were protective; they always wondered if I was safe, of course, when walking. You know, if I mixed it up to keep people from following me. They wanted to know if I had a boyfriend. "Yes, yes, and no," I said to their questions.

Billy said, "You mean to tell me you been up there almost a year and no boyfriend?"

I said, "Nope, waiting on the right one."

They all laughed and reminded me to be careful.

After dinner, I cleared off the table and went into the kitchen to wash the dishes. I walked into my old room, and my Pops knocked on my door. "Hey, I been meaning to send you this mail, but I've been so busy." It was a stack of mail. I told my Pops that was okay and started to take the rubber band from around the mail. The first one was from a college recruiter—old. The next three were letters from George. I opened the first one:

> Dear Lisa:
>
> I apologize for not writing to you, but I have been doing my thing. I want to thank you for making me aware that happiness is not just centered on someone else's dream but your own.
>
> I dropped out of law school, and I am in culinary school. I told you I wanted to become a chef, and that is what I am pursuing.
>
> My parents were not too happy about my dream, but like you said, you have to be invested into your own dreams, and I am. I have so much to share with you and hope to do so soon.
>
> George

Wow! I thought as I lay back on my bed, *George is really doing it. Good for him.* I was anxious to see what the next letter was about. I opened the next letter, and he shared that his grandfather, his mother's father, had passed. He came home for the funeral, and he was very sad about it. He said he phoned me, but there was never an answer, so he decided to write me. After reading this, I felt awful. I understood the value of a grandparent. I could not fathom the loss of mine. I felt bad because I was not there for him. We never know when a friend will come into our life and change the trajectory you've been on. I was so proud of George and at the same time sad. The letters did not have a return address, but I still had the old address. I thought I should take a chance and write to him anyway, and I did.

> Dear George:
>
> I got your letters upon my return home for a visit from school in New York. I am so sorry to hear about your grandfather's passing. I wish I had been there for you, and I hope you forgive me for that.
>
> I am so very proud of you that you are living out your dream. I am sure your parents will get over you not going to law school. I know deep down inside they want you to be happy.
>
> Happiness is important, George. You have finally invested in your future. I have no doubt you will be great at what you are doing.
>
> I'm in my first year of fashion and design school at Parsons School of Design. It's been a learning curve for me as I get adjusted to the culture of NY City. I am following my dreams as well. Can't wait to tell you about New York.
>
> George, I am here for you. Here is my address: 243 Bleecker St., #4438, New York, New York.

I look forward to hearing about everything. You should always know that you are in my thoughts. I wish you the best of luck.

Lisa

I thought about the letters all night long. I wondered how it might have been if I were there to comfort George. I knew somewhere deep inside me that he and I would be friends for life. That's what I wanted, and I was invested in that idea.

Chapter 9

And So It Goes

THE NEXT DAY, I borrowed my Pops's car to go for a visit with my Granny. This was the first time I had gone on my own. *There are some perks in becoming an adult,* I thought. It was so good to drive to the country on a beautiful, hot August day. I wanted to cherish this day and time because there were just certain things you were just not going to see in the city of New York. While driving, I would wave at the people sitting out on porches with families, men driving tractors, and people walking the roadsides after a long day in the fields.

When I reached Granny's, she was waiting outside in the yard for me while watering her plants. I saw a big smile on her face as I pulled up. "Hi, LiLi," she would say.

"Hi, Granny," I replied. I got out of the car and hugged her so tight.

"Wow, you have become a lady." I guess I had because I hadn't seen her since I left for school. "Bring your bag into your room."

I sashayed through the door down the hallway into my room. I sat my bag near the bed and went back out to talk to Granny. "Well, are you invested into your college?" she asked.

"Yes, I am," I quickly said because I understood the gravitas of the question. I had so much to share with her, but I knew none of that would happen until we went to our special spot the next day. My first day at Granny's was a "get myself grounded" day. I just wanted to spend time enjoying her and listening to what was going on with her brothers, their children, and their children's children. It had me saying "What?" so much; a lot to hear about a big family. Granny fixed dinner, and I stuffed myself. At the end of the day, we both ended up out on the porch to watch the sunset with a glass of sweet tea. The sky turned a majestic purple hue beyond any description I could give for its beauty. I rocked in my chair, and so did she. The breeze was running through the house as all the windows were up. When the sunset and I were tired and sleepy, I went in to take a bath. There was no bathroom like Granny's. First of all, the huge bay-like window was so low that you could lie in her lion's claw tub and look out over a pond that was near her backyard. The weeping willow trees waved as though they were dancing to a melodic tune. I lay in the tub with the candles burning, thinking about how blessed I was to be alive at this time, this day, with this woman.

The next day, I was awakened by the smell of coffee and bacon my Granny fixed. There was absolutely no debate about having breakfast at her house. I would eat mine in a tin plate, something I loved to do when I was younger and still loved doing. Good hot biscuits that melted in your mouth, homemade jam, grits with butter, bacon and eggs, all fresh. After breakfast, I washed the dishes and put them away. I went to my room and made up my bed. I looked around to see the old dolls, paper dolls, and puzzles I used to entertain myself with when I was really young. Later that afternoon, she fixed our lunch for our gathering. As usual, she drove her old pickup truck down the road, leaving behind a cloud of dust. We came to our special place. The leaves hung even lower this time of the year as they anticipated the transition of seasons; nevertheless, they provided the same ambience expected—the smell of honeysuckles, the sound of the crickets, and the rolling sound of the water as it made its way to unknown destinations down the stream. I spread the picnic blanket and food. The first fifteen minutes was silence, as she would say, "so you can hear yourself."

Her first question once the silence dissipated was, "Is New York kind to you?" I shared with her that I had some snags, but overall, I was getting adjusted. I told her about Amanda and her family and about Donnie and Greg. We laughed so hard. I told her about Malik, and I shared what happened. She sat me up and looked in my eyes and said this, "Don't ever let anyone make you feel you have to be anything other than who you are. You and only you decide when you want to be intimate with a man. If a boy or man, for that matter, doesn't respect that, then that's your sign to let him go, you hear me?" At that moment, I felt vindicated, and the world was all right with me. We talked and talked and then packed up our things. Granny drove back singing her favorite song "Hold On." That night before I went to sleep and after saying my prayers, I started thinking about my plans when I returned to New York. I had this burst of confidence and energy. I also thought about how George must have felt after losing his grandfather. I could not fathom that type of loss.

The next day, Pops drove me to the airport and walked me to my gate. I was a little sad to leave, but I knew everything I did was purposeful, and so I boarded the plane with hope sitting next to me.

Growing, Growing, Grown

THREE YEARS HAD passed, a very difficult three years at Parsons. At the age of twenty-one and my last year in college, I was steamrolling trying to get all my requirements completed. As a black girl, I discovered during the four-year period that politics weighed heavily on my success. With the input and guidance from Donnie and Greg before they left, I was able to discern whom I needed to know, what groups I might want to assimilate, and what swanky places I might need to be in order to garner necessary contacts.

I met a young blond named Chichi. It's funny I never knew her real name because that's what everyone called her. In my second year at school, she was in one of my advanced designer classes. She was sweet and funny and as wild as they come but not the too ridiculously wild, but nevertheless wild. We became friends because she liked what she called my aesthetic. She said I had the "It" factor, so I just went with it. It never changed me, and I knew I had grown a lot, but even I was curious about this "It" factor that I had. She grew up in a family that had deep pockets: old money. She never bragged about it or flaunted it until we went out, then she would drop a name or two to get us in clubs.

Early one Saturday morning in August 1978, the phone rang, and I stumbled over to it. "Hello," I answered.

"Hey, Lisa. It's Chichi," she said loudly. I could tell she was still out from the past evening. She told me she had met someone, and she told her about my aesthetic and me, and she wanted to commission me to design a dress for her. She said this was a very important person and asked if I was up for it. I could hear several people in the background.

I said, "Yeah, I'll do it." As she was hanging up the phone, she said she'd tell me what I needed to know later.

A week went by, and I hadn't heard from Chichi. I called her without success. On that Friday, a week later, she dropped by the apartment around 6:00 p.m. She said she had partied so much that she had to bear down and close people off to get some shit done. I listened for about thirty-minutes to Chichi's adventures, and they were interesting. She shared this one story about this guy her family wanted her to really like because they liked his family. She said he was cute, but he was not her speed. To please her parents, she went out on a date with him. They would get into the best clubs, and she could get access to the best weed. "When he got high, he was, like, so in love and clingy, you know?"

"Okay," I said, "how do you deal with that?"

She said she played the role but would spend most of the night talking to other people. It appeared clingy was not what Chichi wanted. I asked her, "How do you reconcile that, girl?"

"Oh, I reconcile it because he's filthy rich, I get good weed, and I meet other men that I slip my number to when he's not around, you know."

I laughed and told her she was a mess. I learned that this person I was designing for traveled a lot, and she was an exotic model. Well, that meant she was a black model. She gave me all the specs for her. I needed to know more about her personality. Chichi said she was eccentric, really out there, "so don't be scared to take risks, but keep it classy." We smoked a joint, and I laid across the bed. Chichi fell asleep. When I woke up, she was gone. She left a note, "Had to go, got lots of stuff to do. Good luck. She'll be back in town in two weeks, so you have two weeks to get it done. Ciao." *Well*, I thought, *here is a great opportunity*, but one that would stretch me in all directions as I was working on my final line for the school's end-of-year required fashion runway show.

The next two days, I had my schoolwork pretty much done, just a few final touches. I went for a walk through Revival Fabrics to shop for this woman's material. I saw beautiful colors. Chichi said this woman was darker than myself, and I was chocolate, so I figured she must be a very dark hue; then I should probably look for bright colors that would pop off her skin. I found beautiful fabric, a pink and green striped chiffon fabric. It was perfect. The next day, I went to work on the design, and I actually started on the piece. In three days, I was done, and I took it to school to do the final touches. A week later, Chichi called and said the woman didn't have time for a fitting but wanted us to bring the dress finished to her apartment, and from there, we would go out to a club. My heart fluttered because I started thinking, *What the fuck, what if it doesn't fit? What if she doesn't like it? What if she hates the style?* Chichi saw it and said it was perfect for her. It was a ruffled off-the-shoulder dress fitted with a slit that came pretty far up.

That evening, I got dressed; I steamed the garment and placed it in a bag. I hopped into a taxi to the Hotel Chelsea, at 222 West Twenty-Third Street, between Seventh and Eighth Avenues. I could see the hotel's neon sign far before I got there. When I arrived, I saw Chichi waiting for me outside the hotel. She saw me exit the taxi and came over to greet me as usual with a kiss on each cheek. The hotel was huge. We went in, called up, and then went up. The elevator was tight; we got off onto a dark corridor with marbled floors. We walked to the room, and Chichi knocked. Soon afterward, this extremely tall, dark, and absolutely beautiful black Zulu queen appeared in the door. She signaled for us to come in as she was on the phone. We walked in, and of course, Chichi marched straight to the liquor. I stood there in awe of this woman. When she got off the phone, she hugged Chichi and then was introduced as Grace Jones. I nearly pissed my pants. I extended my hand as usual, but she said she was a hugger. It was time for the reveal. I unzipped the bag, and it felt as though it took twenty minutes to do so because I started thinking, *What if she doesn't like this? This is Grace Jones.* When I revealed the garment, she screamed and started jumping up. "I love it! It's fabulous, my dear." I felt a sense of relief but not totally until she tried it on. She dropped her robe, naked as a jaybird right there, and grabbed the garment. She melted right into the garment; it fitted like a glove to a hand. I was so happy.

We left in a taxi for the club. When we pulled up, there were lines of people waiting; the awning at the entrance of the club had a big neon sign that said 54.

The Ending to a Start

MY DAD, BROTHERS, and their wives were coming to New York for my graduation in December. I was really pumped. I don't think I understood the gravitas of this occasion because I had been busy trying to make sure I had everything completed. The runway show went very well, and my teachers signed off on me graduating. I sat at home looking out the window and thinking about the last four years but more importantly what would the next year bring. I had decided I wanted to live in Paris. Paris was the number one place in my mind to go for an apprenticeship in a fashion house, and I knew if I wanted to become a successful designer, I had to be in the thick of things. I just had to let Pops know that was my next move.

I got a call from Pops; they all had arrived at the airport and were taking a car into the city. They would be staying at the Waldorf for a week. They were so excited for me. Later that evening, once they had settled in, we met for dinner at La Côte Basque. It couldn't have been any more perfect that we were there. It would make it easier for me to spill the beans of my wanting to leave for Paris. It was so nice to see Pops. I ran to hug him, and of course, my big brothers had to make jokes about me looking more like a woman. Everyone was so happy, but as I looked around the table while people were engaged in conversations, I thought how I was so fortunate to have this family. The only one missing was Granny. She did not like to fly. I lifted a glass of water and got everyone's attention. "I give special thanks to my Pops for believing in me, for trusting me to leave home and come to New York on my own. I want you to know I appreciate that trust that you gave me, and I hope I will always make you proud of me. So I salute you, Dad, for believing in me." They took a sip from their glass of wine.

My dad said to everyone at the table, "You all are my children. I love each of you, and each of you is special in your own unique way to me. Your mother would have been proud of you. I know she is in heaven smiling now to see her youngest one happy tonight as well."

Billy asked me, "What's next?"

I said, "Well, I'm going to go to Paris to work."

They all said it at the same time, "Paris?"

I said yes. I had to go where I could get the best experience because a degree alone wouldn't cut it for me. "Paris huh?" my Pops said.

"Yes, Pops, I want to go," I replied. Dobie asked when I was leaving, and I told him I had six months to find an apprenticeship in a fashion house there and also try and make some money "because I'm off Pops's payroll now." They all laughed.

At the end of dinner and when they all went to the bar for drinks, I sat by Pops with my head on his shoulder. He told me how proud he was of me and that he wanted me to follow my dreams. He told me to take the six months of prep time, and he would work something out for me. I knew my Pops didn't have the money Amanda and Malik's parents had or Chichi's, but I knew I had a successful Pops that loved me and would do anything for me as well. I had much comfort in knowing that.

That Saturday was graduation. I saw Amanda, who had come home from Milan for a visit; I saw Malik, Greg, and Donnie; yep, the old gang was back. I looked around and saw Chichi, who waved. I was beyond happy. Following the graduation, my Pops and the rest went to dinner at Tom Wilford and his wife's apartment in upper

Manhattan. Me, I met up with the gang at the Vanguard. It was like old times, but some things had changed. We were older and wiser. Amanda had some of the best stories to share about her life in Milan; Donnie and Greg talked about the boutique they had opened, and Malik talked about making partners at an architectural firm and his pending marriage to, guess who? Carol. Yep, it seemed Carol's family had deep pockets and contacts as well. For some reason, I felt this marriage was more of a convenience for Malik and perhaps love for Carol. You could say Malik was the ultimate opportunist. I was hoping that did not come back to bite him in the ass. I told everyone I would be leaving for Paris in six months to a year. They were so happy for me. Amanda was especially happy because she knew we could visit each other easily, and so was I. The next two days, I went shopping with my sisters-in-law. They were talkers, and not a dull moment was to be realized. I was more of a listener. We went for lunch both times, and they really enjoyed themselves. On that Saturday, before they left, I spent some time with Pops while my brothers went out with the wives. Pops said he would work something out. He said he had talked with Tom, and he thought we could make it happen. I hugged his neck, and we watched TV until I fell asleep. Later on that night, I got up; he had gone back to the hotel. The next day, I met them at the hotel, and the car took us out to the airport. I walked them to the gate, said goodbye, and hugged their necks.

The following two weeks, I searched for a job and found one in the garment district working with this old Jewish woman who had seven young people like myself working as seamstresses. I didn't mind. She was funny, and she talked a lot, but you did learn a lot about stitching. I also learned the business side of the industry. She knew how to negotiate; she didn't take any shit off people who owed her either. She was not to be crossed. She was a short Napoleon complexer; she had a chubby-like body type. She would breathe hard when she walked, almost like she was out of breath. Marisole was her name. Like clockwork, every day she would take a nap at 1:00 p.m. and snore as loud as a wind blowing before a hurricane. The funniest thing is, she would awake and be right back on point. She was fair, but she would work your ass off. I would have to arrive no later than 6:00 a.m. to open and receive the bundles brought in on a truck. The only days I had off were Jewish holidays. I was on a mission, so I was up for the count. We made tailor-customized clothing. Mostly wealthy white people were her clients. Marisole would work your ass, but she would also pay you well, and when she saw you didn't mind hustling, her eyes would light up. I would always realize a few more bucks on payday. She knew I had goals, and she encouraged me. I liked that.

I worked for Marisole for one year. The twelfth month, I had all my plans intact. I had landed an apprenticeship in Paris with Parsons' help; I was accepted as an apprentice under Roger Viveront. Viveront was a well-known shoe designer. He designed shows for even the queen of England but also other celebrities. I was so excited to get my start in his fashion house. My Pops, working with his friend Tom, worked it out and found me a furnished flat at a reasonable price in Paris. It was a one-bedroom flat not far from the Eiffel Tower. I had my passport and working visa as well. This was the beginning for me; I wanted to believe that I would be traveling the road not taken.

The Parisian Way

ON A STEAMY, hot August night in 1980, I landed in Paris, France. When I landed, my heart skipped a beat. I had two carry-ons in the overhead of the plane. I stood up and retrieved the bags. Luckily, my Pops had urged me to ship the rest of my things ahead of time. It took me a while to get through customs. Once I did, things started to move fast. I'd learn most of the conversational French I needed to get a taxi and get to the flat. When I finally came out of the terminal area and waited for thirty minutes for my luggage, I was able to wobble out to catch a taxi. I had a lot of bags. *Wow,* I thought, *my entire life is pretty much summed up in this luggage.* I pushed the cart out and waved a taxi. "Taxi s'il vous plait" and one pulled up fast.

He placed my luggage in the back of the taxi. I gave him the address. He started talking. Then he said, "American?"

I said yes. Thank God he started speaking English.

"First time in Paris?" he asked.

I told him no because that's what Amanda said I should say. She said if not, they would milk me for all the money I came there with; that's what Amanda said. "I'm just returning to work." I quipped.

As he drove, I looked out the window to just take in the beauty of the city. I couldn't believe I was in Paris. As we rode through the streets of Paris, there were a lot of tourists. I could discern the playful energy across the city. People walked holding hands as though they had no cares in the world. The driver pulled up at Rue de la Cometa. He took my bags out of the trunk and walked them up to the door. I pulled out a tip, and he drove off into the sunset. Mind you, I had at least six bags. It was an old apartment building, and there were no elevators. We're talking about a hot, steamy August night here! I buzzed for the building super, and an old, really old man finally made it to the front. I identified myself, and he could speak broken English—enough where I could understand what he was saying. "Oh yes," he said, "voici vos clés et l'appartement est au dernier étage," while handing over the keys and pointing to the stairs and then walked away. "Bonne nuit," he said. I'm assuming he said "Here are your keys, find your apartment at the top" because he kept pointing up. I looked at the key chain, and it said "Sept."

I was saying under my breath, "Please, God, help me get this fucking shit up these stairs." While standing there contemplating how the fuck I was going to get this luggage upstairs in a sensible way, the door opened, and a girl walked through. I said to myself, "No help here." But she was nice. The first thing she asked me was if I needed some help. I was saying in my head, *You think?* "Yes, as a matter of fact, I do." She spoke English, so that helped. We decided to take two bags each and then come back down for the other two. It proved to be a great plan because that is exactly what we did. We were laughing as we climbed the steep, narrow stairs. We actually just sat the bags at the door and went back down for the rest.

When we went back down for the last two bags, I said thank you and introduced myself, and she introduced herself. She was a beautiful girl around my age. She was biracial, and her father was in the air force; she was a service brat. Her name was Patek. I extended my hand out, and like most French, they liked to hug and kiss. She hugged and kissed on each cheek. Patek lived on the other side of the building. "You have the old lady's flat," she said. I didn't know; my Pops made arrangement for the flat. She said I was lucky because the old lady left the flat in great shape. She told me quite a few people in the building wanted that flat. Then she gave me her flat and phone number.

I almost had to crawl back up the stairs with the last two bags. There was one flat to a floor. I had the west front corner view. When I opened the door, it smelled as though an old lady had lived there, or perhaps no one had been there for a while. It smelled of stale lavender. I walked down this long narrow hallway to a huge open space. It was a garden oasis apartment. It had an atrium roof where you could look out at the stars at night and hear and see the rain. It had a small bedroom through a narrow hallway. It had huge bay windows. Oh my goodness! I had the best view of the Eiffel Tower. I stood there for about fifteen minutes just gazing at the tower. It was a dream come true. I had made it to Paris, my lifelong dream. Since the place was already furnished, it made it so easy just to put away my things. The apartment had this absolutely gorgeous white French provisional furniture with the exception of one piece. That piece sat slanted in the corner of the room. There stood a beautiful dark mahogany baroque-style vanity with a huge mirror. The mirror sat inside this beautiful, hollow round vanity top of carved wings. Everything on this piece was carved. There in the center of the table laid a brush, a brush that would remind me of Granny. When I sat at this vanity, I was taken back in time. The Eiffel Tower was the rear view in the mirror. It was absolutely, astonishingly beautiful. It felt like home.

I put away my things, and I was anxious to take a bath. When I opened the bathroom door, it was all things black and white. The marbled tile on the floor was the same tiles on the walls. The tub was a huge lion's claw sunk-in tub. It had a small window that allowed you to crack it open for air. The little pink laced curtains on the window made me think of home. I turned the water on, reached for my nighties from the drawer, and pulled my towels from the linen closet. I sank as deep as the tub would allow me without drowning. After a thirty-minute bath, I sunk into a lovely French mahogany wall bed I let out in the huge living room. The bed was actually a part of the wall. It had a unique bookcase above the head filled with old books left behind. Since the bed was facing the bay window, I could see the

Eiffel Tower. At night, the atrium above gave me a view of nature. It would be about ten minutes of gazing before I closed my eyes.

When I awakened later that evening, I went to the small bedroom next to the bathroom. This room must have been the girl's bedroom. It was everything pink—the walls, the French furniture, and the vanity with a huge mirror, all pink. There was a small closet with shelves for shoes and purses. In fact, a few old purses remained in the back corner of the closet, waiting to be dusted off. I realized I had jet lag, and I knew getting adjusted to the new hours would take a while. The next morning, I awakened. I had to go out and get some food for the apartment. I got dressed and walked downstairs. The old custodian was down there along with a few ladies. I assumed they were a part of the cleaning crew. I armed myself with the little French translation book so that I could have some sensible conversations with the locals. I walked outside and walked a while, but I did not see a grocery store for the life of me. I had to grow some balls and ask. I stumbled through asking where a grocery store was. I ended up saying food. A little old guy pointed and said, "Fauchon, madam. Fauchon." I started my walk, and I saw on the awning exactly what he said, Fauchon. I walked in to find that it was not a store but a gourmet delicatessen. What the hell, I had to have some food to eat, so I shopped. It was definitely a cultural experience. There was a broad range of food from all over the world: Mediterranean, North African, to East Asian. Me, I was just looking for hamburger meat, French fries, and items for a salad for that moment.

While strolling down the rows of food, I looked and there was this absolutely totally gorgeous guy with dimples so deep you could get lost in them. He was tall, dark, and handsome, all the criteria for trouble. He walked confidently, and as he walked toward me, he showed his beautiful white teeth and deep dimples. "Bon jour," he said.

"Bon jour," I answered. I could hear a quiver in my voice when I responded. I kept walking and shopping as well. It happened that we landed at the counter at the same time. I pulled out my francs and paid the clerk. On my way out the door, I saw a man, and I could tell he was American. I asked him if there were other markets around, and he said he didn't know; he was only visiting for meetings. I started down the walk, and I heard someone running behind me.

"Pardon me," it was this hunk.

"Hi," I responded.

"I take it you're not from here."

I told him no, and he introduced himself as Jules Fremont. He walked beside me. I asked him about a supermarket, and he wrote it on the napkin. I told him I'd see him around. As I was walking, I thought and pondered if I had missed an opportunity to meet someone special. When I got the groceries home, I sat the napkin in the bookcase in my bed. I put away the groceries, fixed a nice meal, and started to look at my schedule for work. I saw the job itinerary, and I wasn't scheduled until that Monday; and this was Monday, so I had a week to get acclimated to the city.

There was a knock at the door. I answered, and it was Patek. She asked me if I wanted to do some running around with her. She thought it would be a great opportunity for me to learn the city. I obliged. We got a chance to get to know each other. She was a service brat. She had lived in six different countries in her lifetime. Her dad and mom both were in the air force. She was happy they landed in France because she had always wanted to live in Paris. She was an artist. It was good to hear that because we both were in creative industries. We talked a lot, and she showed me places in Paris I had not even read about. She favored street art, but her favorites were Georgia O'Keefe and contributions to American modernism; overall, she loved Vincent Van Gogh, a post-impressionist. She showed me all the nooks and crannies in the neighborhood, shortcuts to things that could take me forever to do. "Oh yeah," she said, "we should shop at the Air Force Base commissary." Cheaper and I could find more American food.

We returned home around 9:00 p.m. My body was still adjusting to the new time zone. I relaxed and laid across the bed. I called Pops and Granny; they were happy to hear from me. When I reached for my planner, the napkin that Jules had written on dropped on the bed. I unfolded the napkin to read what was on it, and it read:

"Au marche du Marais—7 Rue Sainte-Crox de la Bretonnerie, 7500 Paris, France." Also, there was a phone number beside his name and a message that said, "Call me."

Sense and Sensibility

LIFE MOVED REALLY fast the moment I started my apprenticeship. I went into the fashion house, and the shop was fast-paced. There was so much to learn, and no one was going to babysit me. I took copious notes. I asked lots of questions as well. I was so thankful that most of them spoke English and were willing to speak it around me. There were a few in the house that were not favorable of an American being there, but overall, it was a friendly environment. Design and materials were key to this house. There were seven apprentice designers competing for attention with their talent. It would become vicious. I found myself staying up late nights designing, getting home from the fashion house really late. I was willing to do the work. It would be some time before I met the actual designer, I thought.

Work was going well with the exception of some disagreements with the two Parisians that weren't really happy this American was in Paris. I would often get off-the-cuff comments from them during lunch. Everything shut down at 2:00 p.m. in Paris before they start back working. People take time to enjoy their food and talk. During lunch-in that day, Pete and Andrea were so curious about me. They couldn't quite figure me out; I was an enigma to them. Andrea was very passive-aggressive. She would make remarks that were not only microaggressive, but they also showed how insecure she was. She was tall and big-boned; she had this bottled fiery red hair, and she wore black all the time. One day, they wanted to order in lunch, and I said no. I was going out. She quipped, "It's free, we are given free lunch every Friday."

I responded, "That's fine, I'm going out."

She really didn't like that I said that, so she quickly responded, "Oh, you're too good to eat our lunch, right?"

I said, "Yep," and headed out the door.

That same week, I grabbed my jacket to go out for lunch. Andrea and Pete were sitting in the break room munching as usual on the free lunch provided by management each Friday. As I passed through the break room, Andrea said, "Where are you going?" I told her I was on my way out for lunch, and she boldly said, "You can't go out for lunch!"

I said, "Yes, I can."

She retorted, "No, you can't. You have to eat lunch here."

I said, "No, you have to eat lunch here because that's what you do, you eat the free lunch all the time. I, on the other hand, don't have to. Enjoy your lunch, sweetie! I walked out the door and went to a bistro not far from the fashion house.

A week later, another incident happened. Usually, the daily activities or task sheets were posted with meeting dates and times near the door so that upon entry or departure, each person would know what's going on. That Thursday before I left, I looked at the task sheet, and there was an all-staff meeting scheduled for next day at 10:00 a.m. As usual, I arrived an hour before start time for prep and to acclimate myself; however, when I arrived, Latecia, the fashion house manager, asked why I didn't make the earlier meeting. I was stunned. I asked, "What meeting?"

"Oh, we had a production meeting this morning at eight a.m. with the designer."

"I didn't see a meeting on the activity sheet posted yesterday before leaving."

"Yes, it was there," she said.

I turned to find that a totally different sheet was posted. I could have kicked myself in the ass for that. There was no explaining myself out of a dirty deed that had been done. I didn't want to appear petty, and for some reasons when black folks complained, they would always go there by saying, "Are you being just a little sensitive? We're not prejudiced." So I had to take the heat for this one. That meant I missed the opportunity to meet the designer for the first time and whom I was looking forward to meeting. Also, that meeting was important because designers had the opportunity to present their boards and samples. I missed it. Andrea and Pete were feeling pretty good about themselves for the dirty deed, as to say, "Now you see we run this." I was saying silently to myself, *Okay, this is how it is, huh? I got this.* Later in the day, Latecia came over to my station and asked for my board and materials. Apparently, Roger was not inspired by the designs he saw earlier from the other six designers. I gave Latecia my boards and continued working. About one hour later, I looked up and saw this older man with medium height, blond hair, and sad blue eyes walking toward my station. It was Roger himself. He came to my station and introduced himself. I extended my hand, and he shook it but not before reprimanding me for not being there earlier. I apologized. In his very French English voice, he began to inquire about my designs; he was very interested in my mindset about the designs. I started explaining my aesthetic, and I talked about how that aesthetic was aligned with his signature style. He liked it and told me to keep up the good work.

When he left my station, he also left with my renderings. Pete and Andrea were livid. You could see it in their pensive faces. I didn't think I needed to rub it in at all; the statement had been made. I just simply gave them the middle finger as I passed their station. "You fuck with me, lightning will strike the shithouse, bitches!" They could hardly look at me. All day, both were walking around snatching things off the shelf, walking the long way around to avoid passing my station. I bathed in it. At the end of the day, I was tired but felt good.

It was Friday, and I wanted to do something. Patek was in Milan for an art exhibit, so I was going to either wing it or get some balls and call Jules. I did the latter. I found the napkin and called him. He answered the phone. "Hi, Jules, this is Lisa, the sister you met at the supermarket a week ago. You wrote your name on a napkin and asked me to give you a call."

"Oh yes, I know who you are. How are you?" he said.

"I'm well. I was wondering if you were busy tonight?"

"Wow, it's good to hear from you. I'm open. Let me call you back and I will think of some places to go, okay?"

"All right," I said. I was excited just to get out of the apartment.

It was about seventy degrees, but you could tell the season was transitioning into early September. I washed up and got dressed. He called back and gave me the name where I insisted I would meet him. "There's this unique club called La Cave du 38 Riv." I jotted down the address and told him I'd see him within an hour. I hopped into a taxi and met Jules at this La Cave du 38 Riv. If nothing more, I was punctual. Although I didn't want it to appear as though I was "thirsty." So I walked the block for about ten minutes and wrapped back around to the location. To my surprise, it was a club, a jazz club. The doorman was smooth and friendly. This club was underground. It looked as though I was in a cave. It had no stage, so what it created was the opportunity to become close to the artists. The ambience of the club was somewhat medieval, dark, and intimate. I was a little surprised for a first date at this place, but I ran with it.

Fuck, I still got there too early. I beat him there. I sat at a small table not far from the band. About ten minutes after I arrived, I waved, and he walked over. He reached over and did the French thing, kisses on both cheeks. We chatted for a while before the band started to play. He was curious as to why I was in France. "What brought you to Paris, Lisa?" he asked.

"I'm in fashion and design, and I'm here under apprenticeship with the best," I responded. I told him about my apprenticeship. One thing I learned from my brothers, you don't tell a person on the first date about your whole life. I kept that in mind as I talked.

Whatever questions I would answer, I asked of him. Jules was in finance; he was enamored with finances.

"I used to one day want to leave for New York and become the king of Wall Street," he said with pride. He said he was one of the few blacks in this firm. "My family is from Nigeria and migrated to Paris when I was in elementary school. My father worked as a custodian at a high school to get my sisters and me through high school and college. One of my sisters is a teacher. The other is a nurse." He was really invested into his career. He was twenty-four years old, one year older than me. He liked music, and he liked this place more because one of his clients was an investor.

This was the night I would have my first drink; I just felt like it. I ordered a glass of Château Pétrus Bordeaux, and so did he. He said, "Great wine."

I replied, "I think so," and smiled. I said to myself, "What the fuck." However, two sips and I was spinning. I slowed it up and tempered myself. We stayed there and left for late dinner at a local bistro.

I fucking needed food in me like a pimp needed a whore. When we sat down and the waitress came over, I already knew what I wanted. I ordered a baked potato with baked salmon. When the bread came out, I slowly but effectively broke off the bread and ate it as I talked. "Soak, soak, and soak," I was saying to myself. I didn't order anything to drink. Around 11:00 p.m., I was ready to go to bed. I don't know if it was the wine or what, but I started taking a really good look at Jules. He was really cute. He had these beautiful lips, big brown eyes, and a smile that wouldn't leave you alone. I told him it was fun, but I had to get up early even though it was Friday. I had to go in to finishing off some boards. He was sweet and asked if I wanted him to take a taxi with me. I said no. I could make it there, and I would call him later to let him know I made it home. He hailed a taxi for me and kissed me on the cheeks when the taxi stopped. "Don't forget to call me," he said. I waved and gave the driver my address as I slowly melted into the car seat.

When I got out of that goddamn taxi, I could hardly see. It looked as though the wooziness came back down on me. I walked into the building straight because I didn't want the residents who were standing on the outside of the building smoking to think I was a drunk. I walked straight into the building, and I won't fucking lie, it took me twenty minutes to get up the stairs. I kept stopping and resting every five steps. When I finally made it to the door, I dropped the keys, I bent over to pick them up, and this rush came over me. I opened the damn door and ran to the bathroom. The toilet became my best friend. I finally realized how light weight I was in drinking. I vomit for about thirty minutes. I was so dehydrated afterward I drank water all night. I laid on the bed, and the atrium looked as though it was falling down on me. I closed my eyes, and it seemed as though I was spinning. I prayed that prayer I used to hear Amanda and Chichi pray: "God, if you just let me get through this, I won't pick up another drink." I fell asleep and woke up after a lengthy comatose sleep. I jumped in and got out of the tub, threw on some jeans and a sweater with a scarf, sat on the side of the bed, and fell asleep.

Chapter 14

Snap Back to Reality

THAT SUNDAY, I awakened in full clothes. I had not even turned in my bed; I just straight slept. I washed up and walked to a café to get some coffee. I decided to get back and do some work at home. There was a moment where I remembered that I had not called Jules when I got home. I called him; the first time, there was no answer. I waited thirty minutes and called again. He answered. "Jules, this is Lisa. Listen, I apologize for not calling you last night, but when I hit the door, I didn't realize how tired I was. I fell off to sleep. Forgive me." He was gracious and asked me out on another date, and I accepted.

Three months past and we're in November already. I had gone out on several dates with Jules, and he really exposed me to Paris in its purest form. It made me feel I had definitely made the right decision to move to Paris. Things at work were going well, and I knew I had won the respect of the two who would be my enemies because I knew they hated my guts; and I would never, ever fucking trust them. They were on hiatus, and I anticipated they would try something else soon.

The phone rang, and it was Jules. He wanted to confirm our date. I met him at this quiet but swank little bistro near the Latin Quarters. I had started to develop feelings for Jules. I didn't want to rush anything because I had only been in Paris for three months. But it was great to have him around. We were at the stage of holding hands and kissing in the park. We'd gone on several picnics in the park near the Eiffel Tower. By now I had learned how to manage a glass of French wine. By the way, when I shared how sick I was with Patek, she asked me what I ordered; when I told her the wine I ordered, she looked at me weird and said in her funny voice, "Bitch, you ordered one of the most expensive wines in the damn bar. Your ass was sick because you just don't drink. A two-thousand-dollar bottle of wine and your ass got sick. Something's wrong with you." It was in pure Patek fashion, and I laughed as usual at her sincere humor.

Jules suggested we go to his place that night, and I was okay with it; after all, since I had been dating him, I'd never seen his flat. He waved a taxi, and we rode it to his flat. Life had been really good to Jules. His place had an elevator and a huge lobby. It almost looked as though I was walking into the lobby of a hotel. We got off onto the twelfth floor. When we entered the apartment, it was immaculate, very clean, and neat. He had a stocked bar. I sat down on a plush couch and sank deeply into it. He offered wine, and yep, I accepted. He sat next to me with the wine and drank something a little more manly, I guess. We talked. I laid my head in his lap. We laughed, and sometimes there was silence, and he rubbed my hair. He lifted my head and went over to play a record. Unlike my Victorian portable suitcase record player, he had a console and stacks of records. He knew I liked jazz; in fact, that was something we both had in common. This day, he would play Sarah Vaughan. I thought, *Well played, Jules, well played.* When he sat back down on the couch, I laid my head in his lap again, and he reached down to give me a passionate kiss. I could hardly catch my breath before the next kiss landed. My heart raced, and I forgot how to form complete sentences. I excused myself to the bathroom. I stood in front of the mirror gazing, and yes, I peeked into the medicine cabinet, what bitch wouldn't? I had the sum of three minutes to decide if I wanted to be intimate this night with this man. There was quite a lot to think about in three minutes.

When I opened the door, I looked up and saw him standing there practically naked with his chiseled abs, irresistible smirk, and crystal honey-brown eyes too perfect to be real. So what did I do? I snapped back to reality and walked toward him. I knew I was going to deny this moment, but not before kissing him passionately to lighten the blow. "Jules, I can't take this moment any further," I whispered in his ear. He in turn just held me with reluctant approval. I pulled away and walked to his window. We sat for a while and talked about our favorite jazz musicians. We laughed about the shit he was going through being black and all; you know, the same kind of shit I was going through because I was black too. Later on that evening, I said, "Hey, thanks for a great night, Jules. I'm going to hop in a taxi, okay?"

He looked at me with wanting eyes and said, "Sure, are you ok?"

"You bet. I just think it's time."

He put his shirt back on and walked me down. The doorman hailed a taxi, and when it arrived, he put his hands on my chin and pulled me close with a kiss. "Bonsoir," I said as he closed the door.

When I got to my flat, I let down the bed in the living room, and I sat in the middle of it, legs crisscrossed and gazing out the window at the Eiffel Tower. It had started to rain, so the atrium presented a prism of rain flowing perfectly and serenely. I walked over to my luggage and pulled out a record from the stack my dear brother had sent me, Nina Simone's "He Needs Me." I pranced over to my portable record player, brushed off the record, and played it. I thought, *It's nothing like jazz to soothe the wounded soul.* I undressed and stood in front of the mirror. I started examining my body, imagining what a man might see when he looked at me. Amanda used to say your eyes would never look at your body like a man saw it. She said men were visual, and they looked with lust and imagination. So I knew I would never see my body like a man would imagine it. I went to brush my teeth, still listening to the music. I closed the door behind me and leaned against the wood, panting, aching, and wanting with all my heart to call Jules. I'd never done an impulsive thing in my life, and so I was reluctant to call him, and I didn't. I went with my conscious;

I lay on my bed masturbating and staring at the rain falling on the atrium, and I finally closed my eyes.

The next day, I had a consult with Roger about my new boards. I sat with him and talked about the designs and then suggested fabrics for them. He wanted me to take a trip to Milan in a week to visit the shop there. I was excited about it but more excited because I would see Amanda. I had made several attempts to connect with Jules before going to Milan with no success. While that thought was in the back of my head, that was exactly where I had to file it. This was an opportunity for me to learn the business, and I did not want to take it lightly. That Friday in the office, the other four designers came to chat with me about what to expect on my visit. I learned that I was the first to be invited so fast and that usually it would be a year or more before an invitation would be extended. I felt special, but it also meant I had to make sure I had eyes wide open. I knew, while it was an opportunity for me, it was also one for the two crooks in the office to sabotage some shit.

I made sure that I put my boards in my portfolio case, zipped, and locked it and sat it underneath my desk. I didn't want those bastards to interfere with my work at all. Latecia spoke with me about the arrangements. I told her I preferred taking a train. She bucked her eyes and asked, "Are you sure? You know it's about seven hours, right?" I said I was aware. I wanted to experience the ride on the train first class with space to work on my boards. She obliged me. My train would leave the next day at 6:30 a.m., and I would arrive the same day at 1:30 p.m. I contacted Amanda and told her I was coming to Milan. She was out of her mind happy. She would pick me up at the train station.

The train ride was great, as it allowed me time to work my boards and take in the countryside, listening to the whistle as it sounded from stop to stop. When I arrived in Milan, I was rested because I slept on the train. With my travel bag on my shoulder and portfolio in my hand, I walked through the train station and outside to wait for Amanda. Far away I could hear my name, "Lisa, Lisa." I turned, and Amanda waved me to the car. I walked to the car, and crazy Amanda rushed out the car with the door opened and ran around to hug me. All the way to her place, she was talking about how much she missed the old days and how she had hoped all of us could meet up in Milan or Paris to party. I must admit it was truly great to hear her laugh and for me to laugh at what she was saying as well. I couldn't wait to hear about the fashion of Milan. At best, I knew that fashion in the 1980s were truly cathartic for Italian craftsmanship and creativity. Looking out of the window, I saw Italians sporting hats with ascots around their necks both men and women. Oversized coats and women walking with beautiful Italian shirts tucked neatly down in their pants, cigarettes hanging out of their mouths, Milan had a different culture than Paris. French people were famous for their effortless style sated with that famous *je ne sais quoi*, as opposed to Italians who were masters of translating the art of *dolce far niente* into their outfits—almost a nonchalance look, yet very chic.

We finally arrived at Amanda's crib. It was everything I expected and more. Lit up to the max, it had track lighting all over. Marble tables touted designer totems with exotic accents and chinoiserie and extreme Art Deco antiques. It was absolutely beautiful. She showed me to a quaint little bedroom that was opulent. There was a soft white comforter with plumped pillows. When I sat on the bed, I got lost in it. I sat my bag down at the end of the bed and walked back down this long hallway to another part of the apartment that seemed like another world. There I saw her working space. It was unbelievably huge with swatches all over the floor and workstations with sewing machines all over. It was similar to where I worked but, hell, on a grander scale. "What the fuck? Amanda, you're doing really well," I said.

"I do okay, but I gotta long way to go, girl."

"Listen, I'm gonna take a bath and relax." I whimpered. I pulled my toothbrush and Ivory soap out of my bag; grabbed a towel from the closet, and went to the bathroom. It was huge as well. Lion's claw tub, Amanda wouldn't have it any other way. I took about a fifteen-minute bath and jumped in my jeans and a shirt. When I came out, Amanda had some snacks and a bottle of wine already opened.

"Lisa, have you started drinking yet?"

"Yeah, I'm handling it," I said.

"Bitch, please, by now you should be popping bottles at home," she said. We both laughed as she poured our wine. "So what's going on in Paris? And look, girl, you gotta tell me what's been happening with you. Have you given it up yet?" We both started laughing uncontrollably.

I told her about work, and I also shared with her about Jules. "Well, well, well," she said with a loud voice. "You finally decided to take a risk, huh?"

"Yep, I did. We will see how it goes," I said under my breath.

"And what about the coochie?"

I smiled and said, "Not yet."

"What? Girl, you good!"

I told her it had to be the right time for me, you know. She smiled with approval. She talked with me about the politics of being in the fashion industry, and I shared with her the treachery I had been exposed to already where I worked. We had stories that were similar: the old black tax and never having a day off from being black. Something we knew very few could understand in our two separate worlds of fashion. Amanda shared that her first year in Milan, she had a difficult time because the men patronized women in general but particularly black women. That they did not take black women seriously. "All they wanted to do is get a fuck in here or there, and I wasn't for that shit. If the motherfuckers couldn't see my work as qualifying me for being a great designer, then fuck them, but not literally, you know." I understood what she meant; there was much for us to take into consideration as black women. We were always in *innate survival mode.* That always added stress because we were like soldiers, as we had to always be prepared for whatever was thrown at us, the regular shit you normally get and then the other bullshit because of who you are—black. We kept exchanging stories until we took a nap. We were going out to dinner around 6:00 p.m. or 8:00 p.m.

Later on that evening, we both got up to get dressed for dinner. Being Amanda, she said two of her male friends would be meeting us for dinner. I walked to her vanity and rolled my eyes at her. "Oh, you'll like them, Lisa, just chill."

Thirty minutes later, we were outside hopping into a taxi on our way to dinner, and I was so hungry. The taxi let us out, and we strolled for five minutes on this long walkway under the lights to this beautiful tall building that looked nothing like a restaurant. "Welcome to Ratanà," this tall olive-colored man said. Amanda gave him her name, and he shared that two men were already at our table and led us to the table. Waiting were two other men dressed to the nines and older than Amanda and me. They were gentlemen and stood up. Amanda introduced me to both Antonio and Piero. We sat for dinner, and it was great; the restaurant was pure Milanese fare. They were charming and cute, and they both had humor. That made the night go faster, and I really did enjoy myself.

The next day, I was in a taxi on my way to meet Roger and the Milan shop staff. I made certain I had everything I needed because I didn't want to mess this opportunity up. I walked in, and everyone was busy as hell but friendly. Roger introduced me and talked about my designs. Right after the meeting, I started to sit and observe the designers and engage them about what they did every day. I learned so much from them. It was two days well spent in the shop. I was hyped about getting my feet wet in Milan. That night, Amanda had an event she needed to attend and I didn't want to go, so I hung out at her place. The following day, she wasn't there, so I left a note on her pillow and rushed to the train station. On the way back home, I thought about how nice it was to see Amanda. She had matured but clearly was still the same Amanda, the girl that's going to do her no matter what. I thought that's what we both loved about each other. We never needed approval from anyone to be who we were. I laughed out loud thinking about how it was going to be in Milan when the two queens Greg and Donnie visited Amanda.

Quantum Leaps

I RETURNED TO Paris timely. I always wondered why the trip going always seemed longer than the trip back home. I put away my things and started to think about the trip and how I could capitalize on the opportunities. I had put a drawing table near the big bay windows with a view of the Eiffel Tower. I sat for an hour at the table listening to jazz, sketching, and thinking of concepts. After a while, I thought about Jules, wondering what was going on with him. I hadn't clicked with him before leaving, so I thought I would give him a hello. I dialed his number, and the phone rang four times before he answered. Finally, he answered, and I said, "Hey, you, this is Lisa. What's going on?"

"Oh, hi, there, just kicking it around here with a few guys from the office."

"Oh, okay, didn't mean to interrupt, checking in with you. Just got back from Milan."

"Yeah? How was the trip?" he asked.

"Oh, it was great. It was amazing in fact. I not only loved the opportunity, but I also got a chance to visit with my girlfriend Amanda."

"Wow, that sounds great. So what you doing later on?" he asked.

"I'm just hanging out here. What's going on with you?"

"Why don't we get together later on this evening?"

"Okay," I said, "where?"

He said he'd call me back in an hour to let me know. I started preparing to run water in the tub when I heard a knock at the door. I went to the door and peeped through the hole. It was Patek. I hadn't seen her in a while, so it was great to see her. I opened the door, and we greeted each other with a hug. "Hey, you, welcome back to the world," she said.

"No kidding, we both have been traveling. How was your art exhibit?"

"The art exhibit was fantastic. I sold about ten pieces," she gleefully said. "I was so surprised I didn't sell the pieces I thought people would love."

I said, "That's great, Patek, congratulations! Well, our aesthetic isn't always somebody else's, but those pieces will find their way into someone's home or business. Don't even worry about that," I said. "What else is going on?"

"Just trying to get out of this painter's block phase. I just don't have the inspiration."

She said when she got painter's block, she would do either two things: smoke a joint for inspiration or go to the South of France for a couple of days. A friend of her father, who by the way was a master sergeant in the service, had a little place in Provence, France. Patek said the south of France was due because smoking weed would make her pig out, and she didn't want to get fat. We both laughed. I told her about my trip to Milan, and she was happy for me. She asked me how were Jules and I doing. I admitted that I hadn't clicked since before I left for Milan and that we were going to get together later that evening. She was happy for me. I asked her about her boyfriend, and she said it had been off and on for a while with this guy who had graduated from the University of Oxford, as in Oxford, England. "There is some disconnect with us. He cannot grasp that I am an artist. He wants me to be this cookie-cutter girlfriend that fits in the rim of what his parents want him to have as a mate. I've told him, 'Listen, this is me, and this is as good as it gets, baby!' I told him accept it or not. He worries too much about what people think, especially his mom. I told him his mom needs to cut the umbilical cord, girl." It was so funny because she gestured with her fingers like she was cutting something.

I always tried to give genuine advice, and on this one, I told her, "Follow your heart and your instinct. Your art is your passion. And if he could allow himself, he would see that passion in your art as well, as the passion work hand and hand. You will become successful doing both."

I saw Patek to the door and started back preparing to take a bath. I ran my water and turned my music up. I felt safe to turn my music up because there was only one flat to a floor, and the tenants above or below me seemed never to be at home. After the bath, I laid on the bed before getting dressed and fell off into a quick nap. I was awakened by the telephone. I skipped over to answer; it was Jules. Jules asked me o meet him at this club called Les Bains Douches. He warned me to really dress because he had scored the opportunity to go to this club through his boss's client. When I got off the phone, I became paranoid because I started wondering if I had the right thing in my closet for the club. I went back to the closet and selected what I thought was going to be appropriate. I had these elephant-leg silk pants with a really sleek silk spaghetti low-cut top with a huge wrap. I beat my face and felt good about the look with lots of confidence. I had to remind myself that I was part of the community that set the trends in fashion, so whatever I put on would work for me and fuck them.

I hopped in a taxi and quipped, "7 Rue du Bourg l'Abbé, merci!" The taxi driver seemed to be very familiar with the club. He started talking about the popularity of the club. He said to me, "You must know someone to get into that club,"

I responded back, "I guess I do."

We pulled up to this building with a huge open arch and a face of this man on it. As I exited the taxi, I heard my name being called. It was Jules. I waved back and smiled. I was really happy to see him. As he walked toward me, I could see he had this extremely white Italian shirt—open collar—on with black slacks, a leather jacket, and loafers with no socks on. He reached for me and greeted me with a kiss on both cheeks. We were let into this crowded club of shoulder-to-shoulder people. The floor was tiled, the walls were tiled, and there was a mosaic tile pool with water and people in it. It had a glass Lalique bar. As a designer, I was more than impressed of the aesthetics.

This was a working night for Jules, and I understood it. I wasn't a needy person, so I was almost happy it was so that I could explore the scene myself, and I did. We separated for a while, and I walked around. People were loud and happy, and I noticed the who's who of the world frequented this club. I'm talking about people like Andy Warhol, Mick Jagger in the pool, and everyone just clapping loudly. Lo and behold, as I slowly moved around the hysterically loud crowd that loved something, I could not believe my eyes. It was Grace Jones. She gave a great show in the pool as others followed her. I would surely say hello to her once she exited the pool of course. I looked around, and I saw Jack Nicholson, De Niro, Bowie, and Prince. This was a great night for groupies but for me as well. I had to keep my composure, and so I acted, as I should have, like they were people too. I would always go to that space in my head that famous people ate and took a shit, and by the way it stunk, just like mine. That's a great equalizer psychologically. This club was like a place of freedom. Later on that night, I would discover that it was indeed a temple for night culture; it was cool. Jules found his way back to me and offered me a drink of wine and a kiss on the jaw. With his arms around my waist, we stood there talking.

Later on, I saw that Grace had exited the pool and changed clothes somewhere and was standing at the end of the bar talking. I asked Jules to walk with me. We walked to the end of the bar, and I tapped Grace on her shoulder. She turned and looked, and I said, "Hi, you might not remember me."

And before I could get it out of my mouth, she said to me, "Are you kidding? Hi, Lisa! I don't forget good people. Also, you saved my ass with the dress you designed for me." She hugged me and gave me a kiss on both cheeks. I introduced her to Jules, and I could see in his face he was pleasantly surprised. I chatted her up for a few, and then she gave me her number. I gave her a hug, and Jules and I moved back through the crowd. I was lit after having two glasses of wine. I went into the bathroom where people were expected to be doing lines on the vanity. They were unselfishly offering straws made with fifty-dollar bills because it was that kind of thing. I wasn't bothered by the hospitable gestures but didn't partake and politely said no. I didn't really do cocaine, but I thought I refused to share something someone put up their noses and shared; germophobic I am! When I got back to Jules, it was around 3:00 a.m. and time to go. He said good night to a few people, and we went out the door to the busy street where taxis were pulling up regularly. We jumped in a taxi, and we went to his place. He put my head on his shoulder and kissed me passionately.

When we arrived, he took my wrap and put it away. He gratuitously offered me a drink, and I said no. He offered me a joint, and I said yep. I wasn't a big weed smoker, but I enjoyed how it made me feel. I thought a joint would be a great way to top off the night. He had a cocktail. Off went my shoes, and I sat on the couch with my legs crisscrossed. He sat on the other end smiling at me. Sometimes words don't have a place; they are not necessary. This was one of those moments. Jules expressed he was not going to rush me and that he would follow my lead. I felt comfortable with that commitment. I got up and went into the bathroom where there was an option of a tub or shower. I took off my clothes and turned on the shower. I opened the glass shower door, and I allowed the water to cascade down my back. He came in later. Before he entered the shower, I could see his silhouette through the steamed shower glass, a perfect physique. His cock was hard, but I knew I would not engage this night. I wanted to leave there that night with something to remember the evening, that moment. He opened the shower door and looked at me. I backed up against the back of the shower. He pressed his hard cock against me as he kissed me passionately. I looked at him and said no. I could feel the head of his penis move on its own, it tingled unbearably, and it had swollen. He stretched my arms out and kissed my breast and my stomach. I trembled each time his lips touched my body. Then he touched me with his tongue. I shook with the same intense pleasure he gave me. His tongue was long and soft and seemed to wrap itself in me. Just as I was about to explode, he suddenly moved away to watch me come. He kissed me afterward and left the shower.

I stood there for a moment trying to collect myself. This was different, it was meaningful to me, and I had hoped for Jules as well. I stepped out of the shower, grabbed a towel, and began to contentedly pat my breasts dry. He had left a shirt for me to put on and a glass of wine on the vanity. I pulled my wet hair back in a ponytail, used the lotion I had in my purse, and walked into the living room. He had put on his pants. Soft music was playing, and the lights were low. He grabbed my arm and started dancing with me. No words were uttered. We started laughing about some of the things we had witnessed at Les Bains. By now it was five thirty in the morning. I fell asleep on the couch talking with him. The next morning, I awakened around 10:00 a.m. to the smell of coffee and a comforter pulled over me. It was Sunday. I jumped up and dressed. I grabbed a croissant, gave Jules a kiss on the jaw, told him I had a great time, and headed for the door.

When I arrived home, I could hear the phone ringing as I started up the stairs. I had three more flights to go. I took off my heels and ran the other three as fast as I could. When I reached the door, the phone had stopped. I noticed I'd turned off my voice machine so they couldn't leave a message. I just had to wait to see who it was because I was not going to call Jules to see if it was him. That would have been a little bit too thirsty.

Sundays are essentially sacred for Parisians. Not necessarily in a religious way, although some people did observe it as a religious day like me. Parisians viewed Sunday as a day set aside to amble the streets freely, go to a lazy brunch with friends, go to movies, or go to art exhibits. For me, this Sunday would be spent looking at people's shoes after early church. I wanted to know what the locals were wearing. Yep, I was going to play the role of a fashion forecaster. That meant I would spend it walking the Champs-Élysées and the neighborhoods. I also wanted to spend some time in the Latin Quarters. The Quarters, located on the left bank of Paris, was a different and exotic place to gaze. I was so looking forward to that day.

I dressed and headed back out the door to roam the streets of Paris. I started thinking about the phone call that I didn't get before I left my apartment.

Chapter 16

Unwarranted Guests

I SPENT THE last four weeks keeping busy and designing like mad. I had a crucial reveal for Roger a week out; I didn't want any distractions, and we were only one month from fashion week. I had heard from Jules maybe twice in the two week's time, but to be honest, I was really involved in getting my designs intact. I heard a knock at the door, and I got up to answer. I peeped through the hole, and it was Patek. I had designed a dress for her art exhibit. She came in and tried to pay me, but I refused. "Girl, no, you can't afford me!" I laughed, and she did too. She hugged my neck and said thanks. She left a joint on my living room bed table on her way out the door. I muffled "Oh, thanks" with the pencil in my mouth and "Break a leg, my friend!" When she left, I continued working on my sketches. I had exhausted myself and was famished, so I decided to grab a bite to eat. I threw on a heavy coat and ran down the steps. At the bottom of the steps was Mete. Mete was the old guy responsible for the maintenance in the building. He was so sweet. He never complained if you asked him to fix something in the building. I would always bring him a hot coffee every morning from the café shop down the street, and he would make a big fuss about it. "Hi, Mete," I quipped. "What's going on?" He knew how to speak some broken English, and I loved it that he wanted to speak with me in English. Also, it sounded so cute.

I walked three blocks over to this small bistro to grab a sandwich. On my way out, I caught a glimpse of Jules with a few associates. I walked up behind him, put my finger to my lips to gesture to his friend not to let him know that I was behind him, and poked him in the side. He turned around and said, "Oh wow. Hey, you, what's going on?" He hugged my neck and then introduced me to his associates. One of them I recognized from the night at *Les Bains*. He was a tall Frenchman and looked like a male model. I would never think he worked with Jules.

"Why are you guys in my neighborhood?"

"Well, Renee's (the tall Frenchmen) got the munchies and had to have these French pastries from this bakery," Jules laughed.

"Oh wow, when ya gotta have it, ya gotta have it," I conceded.

Jules asked me what I was up to. I told him I ran out to grab a bite to eat and how hard I'd been working to prepare for fashion week. "Are you a model?" Renee asked. I told him I wasn't but that I was a designer. He was so curious and was halfway a little messy because he cautioned, "We have thousands of designers in Paris, and most of them think they're the next Laurent. Any famous clients?" he asked. I told him whose fashion house I worked out of and that I had designed for Grace Jones. "Oh wow, she's fabulous, the unpredictable Grace Jones."

I immediately responded, "Yes, she is indeed." I told them, "Nice meeting you, guys," kissed Jules on each cheek, and headed for the flat. He quipped that he would call me soon. As I walked back to my place, I reflected on that little gathering and said to myself, "Mr. Renee was an interesting guy." I wondered what Donnie and Greg would think. I was sure people had commented or asked him if he was a model. I refused, especially after his off-the-cuff comment about designers.

Jules and I went out to dinner on several occasions after that night, but most of my time was spent just trying to stay on top of my game and trying to fulfill the commitments of our fashion house for the people who were hyped up about fashion week. We had orders as far as the United States and Spain. Jules knew how busy I had been, so he gave me keys to his place just in case I wanted to drop by after working some nights. I had never taken advantage of it because, well, hell, I'd been so goddamn busy and second, because I just didn't want to put myself in situation where I was looked at like a late-night snack. I mean, I was a liberated woman, but some shit just had to stay the main stay.

Roger had two key people coming into Paris from Milan. It was a big deal for him because one was an investor and the other a friend whom he was making a formal introduction. While he was entertaining them at home, he wanted to make sure his best designers were introduced, so he invited three of us over for dinner. Pete shared that I should dress my best for this dinner because I was going to Roger's Paris house. I didn't know whether to take that as an insult or good advice; seemingly, it came from one of the haters. We had lunch, and Pete dropped some news. He said Roger was an older guy but the sweetest and dedicated person he'd ever met. That was the only thing I trusted coming out of his mouth because I could attest to that. Roger was a great listener and very meticulous. On the way back to the fashion house, we ran into Latecia. She was making a lunch run. She reminded me of the dinner invite for the weekend and said I could bring one guest. Wow, one guest. I thought about it, and I decided to invite Patek. I invited her because she was an artist, and rumor had it that Roger was deeply interested in modern art and interior decoration; in fact, he had done some sketching of unique, inspired fairy-like fantasies. I just thought that would make a more interesting conversation with Roger than finances.

Later on that evening, I dropped by Patek's apartment. I knocked on the door, and she opened it. "Hey, girl." Come on in, girl, what's up? Want some wine?" she offered.

I told her yes and walked the walls of her apartment. She had some of the most beautiful art hanging on her walls. It took my breath away. I was so overwhelmed by the beautiful art pieces on her walls. "Oh, Patek, is this your work?"

"Yep," she retorted in a friendly way.

"You are a wonderfully talented artist, Patek," I said emphatically. "Hey, I came to invite you to be my guest for dinner at Roger's on Saturday."

"Oh wow, are you shitting me?" she replied. I told her I was serious. I didn't tell her about Roger's proclivity for art. We talked about the Saturday and what we might wear.

Saturday morning, I got up late. I wanted to get some rest because I knew I would be up late that evening. I phoned my dad and talked awhile just to see what was going on. After I spoke with him, I called my Granny. She was so happy to hear from me. She was Granny at her best. She joked with me and listened attentively to what was going on with me. As usual, she gave me her best advice. She would end our conversation as always by telling me to "always bring the best version of yourself when you see people, baby." I said "Okay, Granny, I love you," and hung up. I had to call Pete to find out where I was going because Latecia wasn't available, and I needed to know to get to Roger's place. Patek had joked earlier, "If that little bastard gives us the wrong address, I'm going to kick his ass myself." However, he told me I was going to the *Le Marais* neighborhood. It turned out to be the hotspot for many reasons. It was the Jewish quarter, in addition the gay quarter, and also a fashion quarter in its own way. Pete told me his favorite part of that area was the fact that young and trendy designers set up shop there left and right. He said this was Roger's home in Paris but that he had a two really, really nice homes in Toulouse and Provence, where he invited staff every summer for a retreat and to have fun. I was looking forward to going there as well.

My phone rang, and it was Jules. I told him I was getting ready to go to dinner at Rogers. He thought maybe I could come over for dinner with him. Unfortunately, I had to take a rain check on that. I could hear a little disappointment, but he was a big boy, and he could deal with it. I called Patek on the phone and told her I would meet her in the lobby of the apartment building. Twenty minutes afterward, I got my heavy wrap coat and headed for the lobby. Patek was waiting there. We looked fabulous, and we both knew it. You know, just keeping it real. We hopped in a taxi to *Le Marais*. As we rode

through *Le Marais'* beautiful cobblestone streets, stately stone architecture tucked away in courtyards, I felt as if I was strolling through
medieval Paris. It was something I couldn't have fathomed when I
was young. I was really hyped. We walked into another world when
we entered into Roger's home in the heart of Le Marais. The walls
were dawned with really, really expensive art. Patek was in art heaven.
Her eyes were cocked, and her hands balled in a fist as though she
was going to burst. She knew the artist for every piece of art. We were
escorted into this beautiful foyer where a person took our coats; we
took off our boots and were handed, wouldn't you know it, shoes
prepicked by Roger and, of course, designed by him as well. A server
gave us another cocktail, and she pointed us to another room with
an atrium with a view to heaven. There were about ten people there,
some in the industry and others were not. We were welcomed by
a woman whose name was Andree; she was his wife. She was very
fashionable and sweet but quite the opposite of Roger who was an
unobtrusive, modest person.

I sat across from Roger and with Patek next to me. Roger introduced the designers from his shop and then looked across and introduced me to the two men who were the investors. He told them I
was a highly talented designer with great potential in the business.
"Oh yes," one interjected, "we saw your designs, Lisa. They were
fabulous!" I thanked him and talked about how honored I was to
work for Roger. I introduced them to Patek as an artist. Roger's eyes
perked up, and he and Patek talked for about ten minutes until they
invited us back into the conversation. One of the investors started
talking about when he met Roger. I discovered from just that one
conversation that one of Roger's first clients was a woman I held to
high esteem, Josephine Baker. My heart started pumping, and I just
started thinking about how much I adored Josephine, and now to
discover I was working for a person who had honored her by designing a shoe for her, the night was complete! The party was intriguing, and the food was magnificent. Around 11:00 p.m., Patek and I
said our goodbyes as we noticed the lateness of the hour and left to
walk the cobblestone streets, smoking a joint. We were really tripping
about our night. Patek was so grateful that I brought her. She said the

two investors wanted to see her work of art, and she was going to do a piece; he had an appreciation for art. All I could say was, "La nuit a été une nuit que je n'oublierai jamais!" The night was a night I will never forget! We both were really lit.

Before going home, we decided to stop at a local pub near his apartment. I thought we must have had maybe two glasses of wine. There was a local trio playing music; you know, just regular music and folks were making requests. Some of the requests were way out of their wheelhouse. Patek and I would even be familiar with some of the old tunes they did play, and they were amazed. We decided to wrap it up and hail a taxi. Patek started talking about the guy she had this "on again, off again" relationship with. I could tell she really liked something about him despite the craziness he was bringing to whatever they had going. I listened, and I just asked, "What is it that makes the relationship, Patek?"

She looked at me with her glazed red eyes and proclaimed, "He really knows how to fuck. That's important, and let's see," as she rolled her eyes, pondering, "he is really sweet. He just tries to please his mom too much!"

I thought about it for a minute, and I said, "Well, he's not fucking his mama, right?"

We both broke into a deep stomach laugh and took another hit off of the joint before hailing a taxi. It was so quiet in the taxi you could hear a fly piss on the window; it was so quiet. Patek looked over at me and asked, "What's on your mind, Lisa?" I told her I was thinking about dropping over to Jules instead of going home. She encouraged me to do it. "I'd go if it were me. You haven't spent any time with him since your last episode." She needed not to remind me of the shower excursion, a night I wouldn't forget and never talked about with him as well because I was off to Milan after he had taken my breath away. So I let Patek out at the apartment and headed over to Jules, about another twenty-five minute ride.

Since I had the key, I thought, *Okay, I'll just let myself in, and if he's not there, I'll wait for him.* If he's there, I suspected I couldn't keep putting him off, and tonight might be that night. I paid the driver, got out of the taxi, and walked into the building. The doorman knew me as I struck up a conversation with him trying to maintain my ladylike composure. I walked to the elevator, and since this was a first for me, I was a little nervous. I mean, it was the first time I put myself out there and the first time I had the desire to use the key Jules had given me to use. I walked to the door and opened it. I could hear jazz playing as I walked the long hallway, but the lights were out. I sat the keys on the table in the hallway. I thought he probably went to sleep listening to music as he had done so many times before. When I entered the living room, I saw an unfinished drink on the coffee table. I kept walking toward the bedroom and this time called out his name, "Jules." No response, although I heard the shower going. I opened up his bedroom door, and my heart and mouth both dropped at the same time. I said to myself, "Oh, not again," but this time, it was worse. There in front of me stood this tall, lanky male with his dick in Jules's mouth. It was Renee, you know, the tall gal that had a smart-ass mouth when he was introduced to me. They both were shocked; Renee screamed like a woman and immediately grabbed the comforter from Jules's bed to cover himself. Jules, on the other hand, grabbed his pants as I was quickly making an exit out of the door. He called my name and reached for my arm, and I pulled away. I was in shock. When I started running down the hallway, Jules caught up with me. "Lisa, I'm sorry, I'm sorry," he kept saying.

"Sorry won't cut it, Jules. What the fuck, I trusted you." I couldn't even remember getting in the elevator; the only thing I remembered was the doorman asking me if I was okay, then hailing a taxi.

When I got in the taxi, I started feeling sick, like I really wanted to throw up. I was angry with myself that I had allowed him to put his mouth in my private space; then I started thinking, he never wanted to fuck me because he wanted dick more than pussy. I was in a whirlwind of thoughts. It wasn't hurt; it was anger. *What am I supposed to do with what I had just seen?* I thought.

Chapter 17

Recovery

I WENT HOME in shock. I was too embarrassed at that moment to even tell Patek, and I couldn't tell the one person whom I could almost always tell everything, Granny. I was hurt but not the kind of hurt I could define. I considered myself a pretty good judgment of character, and I always wanted to give people the benefit of the doubt. Not in a million years would I have thought that Jules was, well, what the fuck was he? I thought that's what fucked with my mind. We're talking about the world about to be entering the 1990s in a few years, and the 1980s hadn't been too kind to people who were gay.

Two days later and once I got over the shock of it, I was able to tell Patek what happened. Patek was beside herself. She could not believe what I told her; in fact, she thought I was kidding with her until she looked at my face to see the seriousness of it all. After calling Jules a couple of cussing words, she offered me a hit off a joint, and then she started to make sense. "Lisa, what a blessing in disguise that you didn't let him poke you! Look on the bright side of it. You could have had sex with him with probable consequences. You know how the gay community has struggled with HIV AIDS. So irresponsible! Oh my God, I am so glad you didn't, Lisa." That was the biggest aha moment I had ever experienced in my personal life. Patek had been successful in making me feel better about the entire situation. Jules had tried calling me several times, leaving messages on my answering machine, but I never responded. I could not imagine what explanation he thought he could give me to justify what I saw. Nothing and I mean absolutely, positively nothing would justify what I saw in my mind. I had never given him any indication I would accept three people in what we had and for sure not one being a man. I was over it. I had to refocus myself, and like a general in an army, I needed a victory.

For the next two years, I spent every waking moment of my time learning who I was and working to get myself to the level of the efficacy it took to excel in the business. Roger was a great mentor. He introduced me to a brother who understood the business of fashion. His name was Paul. Paul was a Harvard graduate, and his parents were in the service, so he was an army brat just like Patek. I met with Paul to talk about the business side of fashion, as Roger had wanted me to get an understanding of it. Paul was a tall, statuette black guy. He was the most professional and kind brother I had met in a while. He reminded me of Malik. His whole life, he had wanted to be in business, and so when he finished at Harvard, he moved back to Europe to be near his parents first to Ibefa, Spain. And then when they were transferred to France, he moved to Paris. "Paul, I am so impressed with your knowledge. You really explained this to me where I can understand it. I've never been a whiz in math, so at first, I was really dreading to sit with you. What made you focus in finance and business?" I asked.

"Well, my dad always told me anyone can make money, but very few people can manage it. I wanted to do both, make it and manage it."

"Yep," I said. "I have adored my dad for his ability to build and sustain a business. I used to always think my dad was frugal, but he was smart. He didn't buy a whole lot of excessive things unless it was for his business or our home."

"Your dad was smart. He knew that his home was an investment. He probably wanted to increase the value of the home. He was smart, Lisa. I like that." He still was smart about taking care of business. Paul would meet with me the following week. He invited Patek and me over to his place for dinner. We met his wife Kem who was a short, sweet little fireball. She was a psychologist. Patek had so much to talk about because she, like Paul, had traveled the world with her parents. The four of us became great friends and spent time exploring Paris together. Paul and Kem were opposite. Paul was a talker, but Kem was a listener. Our pack joke was when we smoked weed, Kem, who was normally the quiet one, would outtalk all of us. I really enjoyed my friendship with them; I knew we would be friends for life.

In 1981, I flew to San Francisco with Roger for a week, as he moved to the States for a year. We had accrued quite the list of celebrity clients, and a few from the royal family. We had the option to stay in a luxury hotel, but I wanted to experience the natural life of San Francisco for a couple of nights, and I did. Since I was arriving three days in advance, I wanted to enjoy the city. I made a reservation at *Hotel Boheme* located in the heart of historic North Beach. The hotel was an intimate hotel capturing the bohemian flair of the fifties and sixties. I loved the deco; it was *me*. When I settled in, I called Pops to let him know I was in the States and that I arrived safely. I then called Granny to see how she was doing because she hadn't been feeling well the last time I had spoken with her. This time, she answered the phone so cheerfully; that made me feel secure about her health. She would never tell me if she were ill. She just would not do it. "I don't like to worry. Hi, LiLi," she said.

"Hi, Granny, I am in San Francisco for a week," I explained.

"Oh my, you're quite the traveler, aren't you?"

I laughed and shared with her that I was on a business trip but that I was happy to be home for a while—home meaning in the States. I talked a while with my Granny. I wanted so much to tell her about what happened with Jules but was so embarrassed. I didn't want her to think I wasn't' using my brain. Although I knew Granny loved me unconditionally. I thought, *Hold out on that reveal,* and I did.

I had a friend that lived in Frisco; I met him through Donnie and Greg. His name was Tom Jenkins. Tom was the smartest, sweetest person you could ever meet. His father was a well-respected judge, and Tom was a free-will kinda guy. He wanted to make his own path, and he did and very successfully, I might add. I called him to see if we could hook up for dinner. He lived in the Mission District. According to the motormouth taxi driver on my way to meet Tom, they were reconstructing that area for Yuppies, putting new condos and apartments that were pricey. While riding in the taxi, I could see the fog coming in over the ocean. It was a beautiful sight to behold. It slowly covered the city, enveloping it into its mystic ambience. Just like that, the weather turned from seventy-five degrees to fifty degrees quickly. Luckily, I had a jacket to cover.

We met at the Cliff House. Oh, I was so impressed. This restaurant was true to its name. It sat on a cliff overlooking the Pacific Ocean. It was fantastic! Tom and I sat, talked, and caught up on what was going on with each other. Tom had a new partner, and they were doing great; they both were very active in the gay community. His friend was preparing for a marathon, so he couldn't meet us, but it was great to see Tom. The food was undeniably delicious and with the ambience to match. Now that I was managing my drinking, two glasses of wine didn't throw me for a loop anymore, but I knew two glasses were the limit for me now. What can I say, I was on a drinking curve! It was early, and Tom mentioned he had two tickets to a concert, and he invited me to go with him. I accepted the invitation. We went to see someone who was new to me, but I was always open-minded.

It was a packed house at the Great American Music Hall. The artist was Michael Franks. I thought I had died and gone to music heaven. I totally loved this guy. His music was real; it put me at ease and settled my mind. It proved to be a wonderful night. We left the concert and went for cocktails at a nearby dance club. This was my first time in San Francisco, and I did not grasp the huge population of the gay community. They were business owners, performers, in theater, and brokers. They really represented well across industries. They were thick in the bar; both gay and straights were having a fabulous time. When the DJ played Madonna's "Vogue," not a spot could be found on the floor. Once they exited the floor patting the sweat off until the next tune by George Michael's "Freedom" stirred it up again. I was tired from watching. Tom and I were pretty conservative, but we enjoyed watching. By the time the night was over, I had gulped down four glasses of wine, and I was fit for the bed. I gave Tom a big hug and kiss on both cheeks and hopped in a taxi back to the hotel.

The week in San Francisco was an eyeopener for me about business and life as well. It renewed my views about people in the gay community; I needed that. Also, I had an opportunity to sit and just listen to how Roger handled business, how he selected fabric for his shoes, and how he conceptualized designs from knowing women. I learned to determine the price points for shoes, how he prospected for clients, how to plan or collaborate runway shows with other designers, or how to massage new and old clients. It was truly a learning experience. My brain was gleefully busting with information. Roger and I wrapped up things two days earlier than expected, and he gave me an option of going home to Mississippi for two days or spending two days in San Francisco before flying back to Paris. I opted to go home to spend time with my family!

I was so excited to be going home, as I had not been home for almost four years. I made flight arrangements and, the next day, took the red eye into New Orleans and from there to Jackson, Mississippi. When the plane landed and I deplaned, it was hot as hell. I felt as though someone was trying to smother me. It was so hot; the humidity almost turned my hair into an instant afro. Pops was waiting for me once I got my bag. I dropped my bags and ran into my dad's arms. I was so happy to see him. He started talking about how skinny I'd gotten and how tall I'd grown. The most important thing was that he was proud of me; that was enough for me. When we arrived home, my brothers, their wives, and guess what, my Granny were at the house! Oh, I jumped out the car and ran through the carport door to hug my Granny's neck. It was like being a kid again. She had tears in her eyes when she hugged and kissed me. Granny had a nice spread on the table with all my favorites. "Girl, let me put some meat on those bones," she bellowed. "You've gotten so thin by Mississippi standards." We all laughed.

I reassured, "Granny, I eat a lot, you know me. I'm not going to go without a meal. It's just that I burn it off from the walking I do in Paris."

"Wash up and let's eat!" Granny said.

We all sat at the table, and I caught them up on my life from New York to Paris. Their ears were bent to my every word. In my mind, I was saying to myself, "I can't tell you that I have lost out on having a relationship. That twice now I have caught guys I may have been interested in either fucking someone or getting fucked." It was so great to sit and talk with my family. It was a time I would never forget. My brothers shared about their business ventures; my dad gave the real low gossip about the white folks like who's getting a divorce, who was a closet alcoholic, or who was sneaking over his best friend's house during the day for an "afternoon delight." He even knew who were the undercover racists. Between him and my brothers, we had enough gossip to start a newspaper column. Then the infamous question hit the table. "All right, Lisa, who is your boy-friend?" my big-mouthed oldest brother said.

It looked as though all eyes locked on me. "Well, I've had a couple of dates but nothing serious," I affirmed.

"Oh, girl, you are lying," my brother insisted.

"No, I'm not. I am so busy, guys, until having a real relationship is almost impossible."

Granny said, "Leave Lisa alone. When she gets ready for a boy-friend, she will do it."

They all got off that subject, and I took a big sigh of relief. When dinner was over, Granny and I were the left-behinds to get the table cleared and the dishes washed. I didn't mind much because it was precious time I could spend with her. She washed, and I dried them. As she stood there, she looked at me with her big brown eyes and said, "LiLi, you are a beautiful young woman, and I know you know that because your dad, brothers, and I have never given you a reason not to think nothing more. You are smart as the dickens too. But I want you to take time to experience life too, which means take time to get to know someone and maybe one day experience love," she said passionately.

"Okay, Granny, I'm just trying to stay on top because I'm in a business where there aren't many of us in it at the grassroots level. Everything I do or say has to represent us well," I pointed out.

"You're right, and I wouldn't expect anything less from you. But, baby, I do want you to experience how it feels to really be loved. I'm so glad I can say I experienced that once in my life. Your grandfather loved me unconditionally. It was agape love. He allowed me to be who I was, he never tried to change me, and I never tried to change him. We grew together but never apart, and I learned to appreciate what we had with each other. We dealt with what we didn't like, and we found our spaces to do that. That's what I want for you," she revealed. I knew what Granny's experience was saying, and innately I wanted to have that kind of love as well; in fact, I hoped to experience that kind of love. I just didn't know if that would be possible and how. I did know right now I was intent on living inside my dreams.

The next day, I spent time with Granny. Since she was in Jackson, she wanted to do some shopping and go to the market as well. So I made sure I had my flats on because it was going to be a journey. After a day of shopping, we decided to eat at one of Jackson's number one soul food restaurants, E & L. Granny knew the owner's family, and the food was delicious. Lots of folks stopped by our table because they knew my Granny. She would introduce them to me as a proud grandma would do. I looked at her beautiful round caramel face, and it made my heart so happy. That evening it was time for checkers, chess, and spades. Pops invited over a few friends. He was really in his element when his buddies came over. I noticed there was no Johnny Ray. I reluctantly inquired when Pops came to the storage room to get more beer. "Pops, I didn't see Johnny Ray?"

Dad said Johnny Ray was in a bad way. "He has cancer and not doing well."

"Oh," I murmured, "that's too bad."

"Yeah, we don't think it's going to be too long, Lisa, not long at all." Pops sighed. I thought serendipity.

With the gang of buddies there, they would drink, laugh, and lie all night long. Granny hit the sack around 10:00 p.m., and I followed around 11:00 p.m. because I had an early flight out the next day. Around 5:30 a.m., I was up packing and ready to take my bath. I could smell the sausage and the aroma of the coffee coming from the kitchen. Granny would always get up with the birds, so she started breakfast. After getting dressed, I brought my bags into the den and walked to the kitchen to eat with Granny and Pops. It was so quiet, then my dad said, "Lisa, we really were happy to see you, baby. You keep doing what you are doing, and if you need anything, call me. I love ya."

"Thanks, Pops, I love you too," I declared.

Pops left to start the car and load my bags. Granny took my hand and shared how much she loved me. She reminded me of what she had told me the night before. I hugged her neck for a long time and told her I loved her. I gave her a big smooch on both cheeks, ran to the bathroom, and came back through the carport. Dad drove me to the airport, parked, and walked me to the terminal. Before I boarded the plane, I turned and waved goodbye. I flew from Jackson to New Orleans. I had a layover in New Orleans and, around 7:00 p.m., left for Paris.

Chapter 18

Throwing Down and Getting Out

TIME WAS MOVING fast. We had spent three months rolling up our sleeves and following up on orders, evaluating specs, and preparing for fall collection. We were already in autumn of 1983. There is no autumn like a Parisian autumn. Some days were warm, some lukewarm, and maybe a hot day or two; on this day, I just happened to have a day off. I got a call from Roger thanking me for the work I did while I was in San Francisco; I hadn't heard from him for three months earlier. He shared he would be moving back to Paris in two weeks, and he wanted to spend some time with the staff. He reminded me that Latecia was working on the company's end of summer retreat. When I hung up the phone, I sat in the window for a while just reflecting over my life. If I were to give myself a grade, I thought it would be a C plus. I was pretty hard on myself, and I was because I had high standards. I also knew how to give myself a break. But I thought I was driven so much because I remembered when I was young attending an all-white school in the south in the 1970s. I understood the necessity for a black person to sustain a driven modality. As a black person, you were constantly reminded that you were black, inferior, and not smart enough; and even when you were, there was always the propensity to make you feel that you were not worthy. All this bullshit because they knew that white privilege meant a total denial of black suppression. The absolute most denigrating part of it all was the denial by some whites that white privilege didn't exist.

I was happy that Roger was pleased with my work, but I wanted to spread my wings more to see where the creativity would land me. I began new sketches for my portfolio that had nothing to do with shoes. I started feeling a need to look at men's fashion because not many, if any, women designers were looking in that direction. I called Patek over for drinks and to ask her to look at my sketches as well. She would be the best to do this not only because she was an artist, but she also could give me some really great insight through her artistic lens as well. Knock, knock, knock and I went to answer it. "Hey, you," she sassed past me.

"Hey yourself, what's up?" I joked. "Want some wine?"

"Only if you want to share this joint with me," she said.

"That's an even exchange," I quipped.

Patek always had some fire weed, the type that rendered you to silence at least for a moment. As we both sat there looking out the window for about twenty minutes, I managed to ask, "Girl, where do you get this fire ass weed?"

She started laughing, and so did I. "I know right? she bragged.

Well, once I collected myself and actually was feeling mighty fine, I went to my drawing table to get my portfolio sketches. Patek looked at them in silence. She looked again, and then she took the sketches to the floor and laid on her stomach on the throw rug to give them a grand look. I sat quietly before walking over to the record player to put on some music. I put Michael Franks on, as I wanted to formally introduce him to Patek. The moment I put him on, she looked at me and didn't have to say another word. Next thing I saw was Patek on the floor dancing her ass off. "Who the fuck is this?" she bellowed.

"His name is Michael Franks. I saw him while I was in San Francisco, and he is the answer, baby!"

"Yes, the fuck he is! I love this tune. What's the name of it?" she asked.

"Let me look." I took the album cover and looked for the song, and my eyes cocked like a bird that saw a cat coming for it. "You're not going to believe this. The fucking song is called 'Vincent's Ear.'"

"Bitch, you're lying," she gushed.

I laughed and told her I wasn't kidding. This couldn't have been any more perfect at this time and on this day. Michael Frank's song was about Vincent Van Gogh, one of Patek's favorite artist and mine too. She lit the rest of the joint, and we smoked it, lying back listening to the melodious sounds of Michael Franks and sharing philosophical ideals about Van Gogh. The weed helped that conversation along. When we finally came back to our damn senses, it was like twelve midnight. We both lifted, and Patek said, "I need to go, but before I leave," she grabbed my hands, "Lisa, I am so proud of you. Your sketches are blowing me away. They are tight. You've got something special going on, my friend."

I felt great because it came from a good soul, my friend Patek, someone whose opinion I respected and valued. "Thanks, Patek, you don't know how much that means to me." I hugged her; she said good morning and started walking with her hands raised and my extra apartment key that I gave her.

The next day, which was Sunday, I decided after Sunday church I was going to do some me time. I actually went shopping on the Champs-Élysées. As I walked, I veered into the many shops just to see what was new. As I looked around while walking, I would see lovers and potential lovers walking holding hands and speaking a language I had yet to know, the language of love. I envied them in a good way. It was good to see the public display of affections. Deep within me, I wanted to experience that someday, and I hadn't given up hope on doing so. I truly believed that at the right time, I would come to meet the man of my life. Based on my last two experiences with men, I figured out quickly that I had already been to the bottom to discover men were not perfect creatures either, like my dad. What girl wouldn't think that if she has a pretty good dad. I'm not hoping to find my dad in a man but, goddamn, something close to it. I was beginning to view men as accessories; they didn't make me whole or determined my happiness, but they complimented and enhanced what I would bring to a relationship. I had pretty much resigned to that truism because I had two great teachers in both Malik and Jules so far. I supposed I could thank them for teaching me this early out. It could only go up from this point, but if not, I seemed to always bounce back because I wasn't built for being down. I was happy that Paul redeemed my opinion of men. Paul loved Kem. He was smart, funny, and loved his wife. It was always great to be around them. They had what I'd hoped one day I would find. Paul assured me that I would one day; I took him at his word.

Strolling along, I could see lovers unafraid to kiss and hug and look into each other's eyes. Much affirmation was happening because during my entire walk, I saw lovers, young ones and old ones. They all publicly proclaimed their feelings with a kiss and a look. The look was what I started branding it. Before I knew it, I had walked to the Arc de Triomphe. I decided to go all the way to the top. While walking these tiny, little steeped steps, I ran into a couple from Mallorca, Spain. I struck up a friendly conversation with them. They were young, visiting Paris for a month from school. He was French and she Spanish. She told me about the tiny island where her family had lived forever. It sounded so romantic. I knew one day I would definitely have to visit it. He was bringing her home to meet his parents. She had a beautiful smile, and he was lost in it. The innocence of this moment was what stuck with me. I bid my goodbyes and wished them well. When I reached the top, I could see all over Paris, the Eiffel Tower, and even my flat. I thought, *Paris is for you, Lisa, just like you are for Paris.* I finally reached my apartment after a long day of discovering Paris because you never stop doing that no matter how long you've lived there.

On that Monday in the shop, everyone was talking about the upcoming retreat. Since I was the new staffer, I could only listen and hear the many stories about staff on the retreat. There were some interesting stories of late nights in the pubs, people hooking up, and how one or two drunk people got so blasted they started talking truth talk. At least my Granny used to tell me about truth talk. That's when someone got drunk, they would start really saying what's really on their minds, and it's usually the truth. Oftentimes it could get you in trouble, as my Granny would always say. Anyway, I was listening to staff with, I must say, a great sense of anticipation. Roger had two places in France, one in Toulouse and the other in Provence. However, staff would be traveling to Provence this year. This was a switch for the staff, as they were accustomed to Toulouse. There was great buzz about what to expect in Provence. I was really excited! I didn't want to seem amateurish by asking what to take as far as clothing, and I did not want them to feel they had to inform me because I had not been exposed, so I would have to wing it.

In our staff meeting, Latecia mentioned we would be on this retreat with Roger's staff from Milan, the US, and France. I thought, *Wow, this is huge.* So while everyone was chatting about having a good time—and believe me, I wanted to have one as well—I was thinking about what to wear while there and who I needed to meet from the other locations to learn something about the business. We had three weeks before we left for the retreat. We had an option to travel together or make our own reservations. I had to think about that one because I pretty much wanted to do it alone, but I had to think smart. This was also a time to show I could really be a team player. I decided to have Latecia make the reservations with staff. I knew that the average travel time between Paris and Provence was four hours and twenty-seven minutes. The first train would leave Paris at 7:19 a.m. and the last at 9:19 p.m. Latecia called me and asked if I didn't mind taking a later train. She explained because she couldn't get us all together, and while there were six trains leaving daily in two-hour intervals, they were all packed. I knew the motley crew had pitched for the first tickets, and that was okay. It was also wine season, and people from all over were traveling to the vineyards. It was almost a dream come true. I said, "Oh, for sure, not a problem. Just be sure to leave me an itinerary." She told me a car would be there to pick me up at the station. So I took one for the team but at the same time got what I really wanted as well. This trip had really started out great for me.

Three weeks came and went, I commenced packing two days in advance to give myself an opportunity to make any changes I needed to and not to leave anything behind. I was a light packer, but I was a methodical packer. I usually had everything I needed. I packed my portfolio as well, and I thought, *You just never know, right?* The others had departed, and I had some time at home to settle down and brace myself for the unexpected. I was a little nervous. It was obvious that I would be the only black person on this trip. I was hoping that by some miracle, there would be another black person coming from Milan or the US. The fashion industry welcomed black models, but it was not too kind to blacks wanting to dip their toes in the magical part of the industry at all. They would exploit our bodies but not our minds. Not welcoming at all. However, I had met two people who were black in Milan and three in the US. I had always been able to block this out because I was busy trying to master the black tax. You know, the notion that black people had to work and perform regular tasks twice as hard as white people. It was real. My dad always pointed that out to me as he fought his way to becoming respected as a contractor. Oh yeah, you couldn't be too professional either, or you'd be gleaned as an uppidy nigger. You were damned if you do and damned if you don't, no gray space at all.

I could remember, when my Pops first started his business, he had about three white guys working for him because it gave white folks some okay conscious approval. It was a smart business move. When he would bid for big jobs, he would prep and send one of his white contractors to secure the contract. Early out, he would visit the sites for inspection and approval of work. Sometimes when he visited the site, owners would ask who he was or act as though they would rather talk with the white man rather than him until they discovered he was the boss. That was a smart move, and he did this until he accrued a sizable clientele. My brothers experienced the same as they fought to become entrepreneurs. My brother Dobie, in the communications industry, had a hard way to go to become the first black to own and operate a radio station in Hattiesburg, Mississippi. My brother Billy had an easier tax; he mostly dealt with finding a prime location for his dental practice. Oh yes, I was very aware of the black tax. I was hit with it while in school and even now. I remembered when I arrived in Roger's fashion house, Pete and Andrea had their own set of assumptions about who I was. They wanted to right from the first day establish that they were better than me just because and, secondly, just because I was black. I still didn't trust them because they were only courteous to me because Roger liked me. I thought of them like my Granny use to say, "I don't trust them any further than I can throw them." Period.

The day of the departure, I arrived at the train station one hour prior to departure. It was crowded more than usual. It was the wine season, and people from all over the world were on a pilgrimage to the vineyards. As I boarded the train, I saw happy faces of people who were on their way to the vineyards. I met an older couple from Lyon. They had been vacationing in Paris for a week at their son's place. They glowingly talked about their grandchildren. I saw pictures of little kids with puffy jaws. I listened attentively because she reminded me of my Granny because I saw grandma love in her eyes. I also met a couple on their second honeymoon. They had wanted to go back to Provence where they met and fell in love, but having four children and raising them to become independent kept them busy. Now they could go again, and they were looking forward to it. It was a welcoming experience to meet and talk with so many people who were just happy. Each time I shared I was on my way to a staff retreat, they would say, "Make time to have some fun and taste the wine."

When the train arrived, and as Latecia promised, a van was there to drive me out to the countryside. The sun had sat as I arrived late. Since I was the last to arrive, it worked out for me. I ended up staying in Roger's coach house, at least that's what we called it in America. Most of the other staff stayed in famous photographer and film director Agnès Varda's estate, which wasn't far from Roger's place. Roger's wife greeted and welcomed me. She kissed both my cheeks and asked if I was alone, and I answered yes. She said okay. It dawned on me that I could have invited a guest. I didn't have anyone to invite because Patek was on holiday with her boyfriend and I didn't have anyone. So this was going to be a once-in-a-lifetime experience for me, one that I would enjoy immensely.

Their home was absolutely beautiful. I immediately said to her, "What a lovely home." She said she would give me a tour as soon as I settled in. She escorted me through her house straight to the back where there was a huge cobblestone driveway that curved in front of a coach-like house and a pathway that led to a wooden gate. When I entered the coach house, I entered through a kitchen, and through the kitchen was a tiny bileveled living room. She gestured to sit my bags down and come with her. I obliged her. We walked back through the back entrance. She gave me a tour of the main house; she explained it was a stone house built in early 1970 and was designed in the cottage style of the Normandy region of France. She said it was custom-made for the house, the roof tiles were manufactured using fifty-four subtle different hues; she knew I could appreciate that tidbit of information. Still, my favorite part of the house was the books in the window and the pots on the porch. Simple yet that was what made their home appealing to me. I thanked her for the tour and excused myself to the cottage. Upstairs was nice and quaint. A lovely French bed with beautiful white comforters and soft feathered pillows stood in the middle of the room. The window reminded me of a bay window because it was huge and you could look out at vineyards far away from the cottage. As the sun was dismissed, the moon shone down brightly with its contrasting blue shining on the dark and dusky purple shades of lavender that I could see for miles. In the corner was a wet bar with a bottle of Chateau d'Esclans with a wine decanter, cheese, and crackers.

When I unpacked my things and placed them in the drawers, I went to the bathroom too and stepped into second heaven. There stood a lion's claw tub you could get lost in for days. There was a French sink and lots of bubble baths and soaps. It had candles that smelled of lavender. It was a dreamy place to be, and I immediately took advantage of it by running a hot bath before lighting the candles. On the bed lay a welcomed note and itinerary from Latecia. We had an early start for breakfast and a "get to know you" type breakfast at that. I was *really* looking forward to that...wink, wink.

The Reunion

THE NEXT MORNING, I bounced out of bed and went for a quick bath around 6:00 a.m. I looked out of the bathroom window to see what the scenery looked like during the day. It was just as beautiful during the day. Rolls and rolls of lavender. I thought, *What a stunning autumn day.* I closed my eyes for a few seconds to take it all in. I finished dressing by 7:30 a.m. I grabbed my writing tablet, pen, and purse and headed down the stairs. When I went downstairs outside the door, the houseman directed me toward the cobblestone walk that led to the dark-green wooden gate. I opened the gate, and there they were. The majority of the staff from Milan, France, and the US was standing around chatting. A server met me with a glass of juice, or so I thought. When I tasted it, to my surprise, it was a lovely glass of mimosa. *What a great start,* I thought. I walked the floor to get to know everyone. Too many names to remember, I tried to discern who were the ones I needed to know as I talked; it was a process of elimination. Most of them were very friendly. Like I expected, Pete and Andrea were gathered in the far corner talking with three equally insecure look-alikes. But I wanted to fuck with them, so I walked up to them and extended my hand for a friendly shake and introduced myself. The shock on their faces spoke volumes about how messy they were. One of the gay guys said, "Oh, *you're* Lisa!"

I mused, "Yes, and you are?" Ignoring the sarcasm, he was dishing out too early in the morning. "Nice meeting you," I quipped and walked away. I could feel the daggers in my back. It also lifted me because I always had the belief that it's never good to allow anyone that much space in your head. The day was going well for me.

Roger called us all together and welcomed us to his cottage and to Provence. It seemed we were lucky because it was the lavender harvest season. He gave a quick background of the season. It appeared that harvesting and distillation of lavender took place from the start of July to late August; during this time, they would showcase Provence's lavender distillation techniques. We were so lucky because we were going to be attending the annual lavender festival that evening. I pondered, every day I had lived in France, I'd learned so much more about its beauty. I thought wine and fashion were the mainstays for France, but now I'd learned about the lavender—another reason to love this country.

Lunch was catered in. We didn't stop for lunch until 11:30 a.m. We had a salad and soup with pâté as an option. The main course was fish with potatoes, rice, pasta, and a vegetable. There was also a cheese course and dessert with lots of bread. The French really loved their bread. I learned that when I ate the bread, I didn't get as hungry throughout the day. I thought I discovered the secret to why there were not many fat French people! The rest of the day was about the business. I listened attentively to representatives from the different houses because I wanted to learn as much as I could. I just soaked it all in. During the breaks, I drank wine and asked questions. They were always curious about me because I was black, about my hair, about where I lived in Paris, and about what type of family I came from. So I used that to my advantage. They wanted to know about me, so I thought it was an even exchange to enter into their space to learn. They weren't always interested in me just because I was black, but I felt it was because I was black and in the fashion industry, an industry that usually excluded blacks unless you were a model. That in itself was not right, and it always made them, I thought, suspicious and nervous.

We were done by 3:00 p.m., and everyone departed to where they were staying. Our itinerary noted we had to meet in front of Roger's cottage to take a van over to the festival and to dinner at 5:00 p.m. as well. I took time to freshen up and relax. It would take us about fifty minutes to get to the village where the festival was and the restaurant as well. Our plan was to get dinner first and then split up for the festival. No one had attached to me yet. I guess I could understand that because they all were in the same location, so they kinda bonded with one another. I was also cognizant for them; to do so would mean they would have to make themselves comfortably uncomfortable. I kind of felt that the American designers were hesitant to engage me because they didn't want to validate a black person; that just might not be smart. I was all right with that. I sat by Roger's wife in the van. She was very talkative, and her English was broken, so it was always interesting to hear her talk. She raved about the restaurant we were going to. She said she had been there many times, and she had used them for catered occasions. She raved about the chef and the food. I was happy to hear that was one thing I didn't have to worry about, if the food was good or not. Black folks don't care where we go; we wanted to eat good food.

I was famished, but I also knew that to eat in France is to sit for at least two hours, so I paced and braced myself. The French took their time eating, no rush. They believed in savoring the food and the company as well. It was going to be important for me to jockey myself near someone who was talkative and someone I wanted to hear talk. I chose Latecia because she was talkative and I kind of wanted to catch up on what was going on. So when we entered the restaurant, I would have to make sure I sat at Latecia's table. The van stopped in front of this fantastic hotel that almost looked as though we were stepping into another century. We entered the hotel lobby and then the restaurant. There were white tablecloths that laid on each table, fully dressed in silverware and glassware. The room was stunning as we were escorted to our table. They were expecting us, so there was a long dinner table to seat about twenty-five people. Latecia was a pro at this. She knew to sit near the end of the table, and I sat right across from her. I liked Latecia. She was a smart worker and very loyal to Roger. She was also friendly and genuine. Her mom died months before I arrived in France. Roger told me she had been keeping herself busy, and he worried that she had not taken time to grieve. I was always mindful of that, and so I showed her respect and gave her space, you know; I didn't act like some brat that needed her to do everything for me, as I had witnessed.

We sat for dinner, and of course, it was always theatre when you were at dinner in France, especially if you were at a very famous restaurant, and we were: L'Oustau de Baumanière. If the food was anything like the service, I was in for a great evening. The sommelier was knowledgeable about the wines and entertaining to boot. The menu was in French, and I had learned a little French, but my confidence wasn't really at one hundred. Also, that night, I would be tested. I was thinking, if I fucked this up, I was going to be eating a bunch of shit I didn't like. I had to give it a go, so I did. When the server came to me, people almost purposely ignored me as though they didn't want me to feel embarrassed. But of course, Pete and Andrea were tuned in to see what I would order. I started my order, "Monsieur, j'aurai calamar spetits et grands, feuilleà feuille de cochon, arteaux petitspois, focaccia, beau et déjeuner aux baux, merci!" I smiled and engaged Latecia immediately in a conversation as she went on and on affirming what I ordered would be delicious. When I glanced down later at Andrea and Pete who were locked in on me with amazement and envy, what I really wanted to say was "Now, bitches."

The night went on, and the food was just absolutely to die for. After two hours and things were turning down, Roger asked to see the chef. The server obliged him. Five minutes later, the chef came out standing behind me but facing Roger. Roger said to him in French, "La nourriture était magnifique, et merci pour le merveilleux repas."

He replied, "My French isn't as good as yours, but thank you. I'm glad you enjoyed the food, merci."

Roger repeated in English as they both laughed, "The food was magnificent. Thank you for your wonderful meal." Everyone clapped. When I heard the laugh, it was a familiar laugh to me. I had to turn to look, and when I did, I almost fainted.

Chapter 20

Again

I TURNED AND looked straight into George's eyes. He looked in mine with disbelief as well. We said our names simultaneously. "George?" I chortled.

"Lisa?" he blurted.

"Wow!" I said. "I'm so happy to see you!"

"Lisa, I can't believe it!"

I got up from the chair, and we embraced each other. You could hear a cat lick ice; it was so quiet from the guests at the table. George and I kept staring at each other until I caught myself and gave an explanation to the guests. "George and I are friends from long ago when I was a teenager and so was he. We haven't seen each other for a while as you can tell, yes?" I asked the guests to excuse us, and I stepped away from the table and walked outside into the open terrace to chat with him.

George confirmed, "I am so happy to see you, Lisa. I was baffled because we stopped communicating—"

I stopped him by putting my finger on his lips to assure him I understood. "We've got a lot of catching up to do, years of catching up, George."

"How long are you going to be in Provence?" he asked.

"This week, I know for sure. I'm here on a staff retreat."

"Can we get together maybe Wednesday this week?" he asked.

"Why not? I'd love to."

I told him where I was staying, and he knew exactly where it was, as he had been there many times. "Let's say 8:00 p.m. I'll pick you up, yes?"

"Sounds great, George. I'll see you Wednesday."

He gave me a peck on both cheeks while holding my hands. His smile lit up the night. I walked back to the table where my guests were waiting for further explanation. But what I realized was they wanted to know what George meant to me. Roger quickly changed the subject by taking it back to the marvelous food he had eaten. I was saying to myself, "Thanks, Roger, for rescuing me on this one." He looked at me across the table with approving eyes as though he knew exactly how I was feeling.

We headed to the lavender festival. I was really curious about what we were going to do at a lavender festival late evening. On the ride to the festival, I couldn't help but smile every time I thought about seeing George. I had wondered often where he was and if he was disappointed that I was not there for him when his grandfather passed. I only felt that way because I highly valued my Granny, and I would probably want my friends to be near me if I lost her; the pain would be too much to bear. I was looking forward to spending time with him. When we arrived at the festival, it was the most unique thing I had experienced since I was in France. We agreed to meet back at the main area at a given time, and we all split up with the exception of those who wanted to go in groups. The moon was so bright that night that when looking at the fields as far as you could see, it looked as though it was resting on the rows of lavender. There were small blue and white lights that lined the rows to guide guests through the rows of lavender. It was almost like a ritual, as people from all over the world converged onto the rows of the lavender fields. The smell was unbelievable.

I chose to go it alone. After all, I was on a natural high after seeing George. As I walked the rows, if you could believe it, each row had a deeper and different smell of lavender. It was the most calming walk ever! I enjoyed people watching as I walked. Typical France, couples would stop and kiss as they strolled the field. I envied them because I could imagine sharing this experience with someone I really loved. It had to be the maximum. I walked for about thirty minutes but headed back toward the front because I wanted to take advantage of some of the souvenirs in the small shops and food stands as well. When I reached the front, I stopped at the lavender dessert stand. I bought a lavender lemon bar, honey lemon ice cream, and a small cup of lavender ice cream. It was way more than I expected. It was delicious, and I thought, *Leave it to the French to have lavender ice cream.* An hour had passed, and when I glanced up, I could see the van pulling up. The others started loading, so I joined them. I was exhausted, as it had been an eventful night.

Roger's wife talked the entire ride back to the cottage. The others were chatting about going to a local pub, but I knew I wasn't going to make it. I was elated to hear Latecia say she was tired as well, so I affirmed it was a long day and anticipated early morning. I joked with them and wished them a happy time. When the van let Roger, his wife, and me off, I said good night, and I walked around the house on the cobblestone driveway to the cottage. I went upstairs, drew a bath, and afterward jumped into bed. That Wednesday, we had a long day session and were given free time for the evening on our own. I was invited by my team to go to a local Parisian pub, but I reminded them I would be seeing George that evening. It was a very warm autumn night, and I had to wear something that was cool but cute as well. I had this beautiful spaghetti-strapped white cotton dress that was short because I was proud of my beautiful long legs. I wore these beautiful Italian sandals I bought while in Milan. I sprayed on my best perfume, put my hair in a long ponytail, beat my face just a little, and put on clear lip gloss. I felt pretty; therefore, I was.

Around eight o'clock, Roger knocked on my door to let me know George was there to pick me up. I grabbed a shawl and purse and headed for the door. Roger told me to have a good time. When I walked through cottage to the front, I saw that beautiful smile on George's face. "Hey, you," he said.

"Hi, George."

"You look beautiful!" he exclaimed.

"Thank you," I responded.

He opened the door for me and walked to his car door and opened it for me. I started feeling bubbles in my stomach. I felt like a teen going on my first date. When he sat in the car, he said, "I just have to pinch myself because I can't believe I am with you in France."

I laughed and quipped back, "Well, go right ahead, or do you want me to pinch you?"

He blurted out a laugh. He told me he hoped I approved of his plans for the evening. We chatted a little in the car. I told him I was sorry I missed going to his grandfather's funeral. He said I wouldn't have known, so I didn't have to bother apologizing for that. I started talking about my move to New York. He mentioned he had gotten the letter I sent him and that he brought the letter with him in hopes to write back to me. We drove for a while, then we finally pulled off the road down a long, dark dirt road that ended with a view of the cutest cottage draped in greenery and lavender. The cobblestone driveway led to the door of the cottage. Behind the cottage, I could see these huge trees that moved with the breeze. George came around to open my door and to help me out the car. He took my hand and led me to the door. "This is a small cottage I bought two years ago," he explained. When we walked through the door, it had a masculine but neat appeal to it. The living room was small, but as we moved toward the back, it opened up into a huge kitchen that led to an open wall and a step-down patio made of stones. There in view was a long wood table with benches on both sides. Beyond that was a gigantic yard and a pond beneath those humongous white oak trees. It took my breath away.

George opened a bottle of wine and announced he was going to prepare dinner. I asked if I could help, and he said, "No, because then I can't impress you, right?" We both laughed, and I sat outside with my back against the bench and my eyes toward the sky. I walked down to the pond and sat on the bench there. For the first time, I felt a piece of home; I was talking Mississippi home. Maybe it was the pond and the big white oak trees that reminded me of the sycamore trees near my Granny's house and the quiet moments that made everything all right for me. I felt safe and special. Fifteen minutes later, George came out with picnic blankets and baskets. He laid the blankets and baskets down and went back for more. On his way back, he walked backward as he smiled at me. In his absence, I gazed down at the pond, and tiny lights flashed on and off while hovering over the patches of wildflowers climbing up the pond's bank, fireflies lighting up the night. On another trip out, I asked if he needed help, and he said no. When he returned, he brought cloth napkins, glassware, utensils, wine bottles, and glasses. Finally, he came back with candles, a cheese course, bread, and the main course as well.

When the circuses were over, it was time for us to enjoy our evening. We sat on the blanket as he replenished our wine glasses. "So tell me," he said, "what have you been doing, Lisa?"

I started telling him about my move to New York and my friends. I talked passionately about the Vanguard jazz club and whom I had seen there as well. He was taking in every word I spoke. I spoke much about my career and how I was carving my way through it step-by-step. I turned the tables and asked him the same question, "What have you been doing, George?"

He started to explain what he had gone through after he disappointed his parents after announcing he wasn't going back to law school. He said it really fucked his mind up because he cared about how his parents thought about him. "I feared I was disappointing them. I felt that extra pressure to become successful as a chef," he said. "My mom was disappointed more than my dad. Dad pretty much said he would support whatever I decided to do."

When we finished eating, he poured another glass of wine and took away some of the picnic accoutrements. While he was gone, I laid flat on my back just looking up at the sky and listening to the wind blowing through the trees. When he returned, he laid beside me, and we started reminiscing about when we were younger. "I was so surprised that you talked to me at the pool," he said.

I asked, "Why?"

"Because I had Southern grandparents that always painted the picture of separation of the races. I knew the South was different, but I also knew I felt and thought differently as well."

I told George my dad raised me to feel comfortable engaging anyone. I wanted him to understand that unapologetically I was a black person that was fortunate yet still victimized by the bullshit decisions his ancestors had made. At this point, I wanted to see if George was cognizant of his white privilege and how that made a difference in our two worlds. He listened attentively to me as I spoke. I wanted to know his thoughts, and so I asked him directly, "What are your thoughts about me being black and you being white?" What I did not want to hear from him was the adage that many white people give, "I don't see color," because that would have been a deal breaker first; and secondly, the question whether we could have a friendship.

He looked me in the eyes and said, "I can never know how you feel being a black person, Lisa. I can only try and understand it by communicating with you. I will never know how it feels to be treated rudely and vile just because of my skin color. But what I can do is not treat you or other blacks that way and certainly not entertain friendships with others who can't respect you."

In that moment, I said a silent "Yes! That's a starting point." I shared with him some of the things my dad had gone through as a black contractor in Jackson. His ears and eyes were wide open as he listened and asked questions. He leaned over me and kissed me on the forehead and said, "I'm sorry you and your dad had to experience that." He confessed, "You mean a lot to me, Lisa. I will never disrespect you, your family, or any blacks because I have been living in a different world than you, understand?"

I gestured yes by nodding my head as I lay on my back looking in his eyes. I told him it was getting late, and I had an early meeting. He made me promise that he could pick me up Friday to spend some time with him. "I want to take you to a village, okay?" I promised him, and then I helped him gather the rest of the things for the house. On the ride back to Roger's cottage, he asked more about my work, and I asked about his. He asked about my Granny, and I talked about my trip back to the States to San Francisco and Mississippi. It was rewarding to see that we both had landed in a space we wanted to be in. The only real thing now was to make things happen in those spaces.

The next two days at the retreat, we really rolled our sleeves up to work on some plans for the upcoming fiscal year. I had a chance to show my sketches that I hadn't even shared with Roger. The shoe sketches were unique, and they were aligned with Roger's aesthetic. The Milan staff in particular was impressed with my work. I also saw other staff's work, and their shit was tight. It affirmed I was on the right track but that I needed to up my game, and I was ready for the challenge. That Friday was an easy day; in fact, we had pretty much wrapped up the retreat, but everyone's departure times were at their desire. The retreat wasn't officially over until Saturday evening, which was leisure and on-your-own time. I was really looking forward to spending time with George that evening. I rested and took a nap after a long bath. I slept for two or more hours. I awakened to an autumn shower. I loved the rain because it comforted me. I had often been drawn to the harsh weather of wind and rain, either to celebrate it as a force of nature or to lament its ubiquity. It reminded me of a poem I memorized that expressed my deepest thoughts about the rain.

Have you ever felt the rain
To some, it brings
Joy and pleasure
To others, it brings only pain
Over the hill, I watched it come
I had my choice, I could have turned and run. I felt it
Fall all over me for that while; it was everything
I hoped it would be until all at once, it stopped
It left me dumbfounded and absolutely shocked
I had never felt so much joy nor have I felt
So much pain now at the end of
Every day
I'm wishing, wanting, and waiting for the rain
—Unknown

Right on time, George picked me up, and this time, I was waiting for him to avoid having Roger come and retrieve me. I stood in the midst and leaned back, absorbing it with pleasure. He had a white Italian shirt on with jeans. "My, my, my," I said to him. "You look great." He returned the compliment, and then he started telling me where we were going. He warned me it was a long drive, but it was worth it. I agreed. I said in a laughing tone, "I might have to make a bathroom stop. Are you okay with that?"

He laughed and said, "For you, yes, Lisa." He had a CD player in his car, so we listened to jazz and talked about the musicians. He told me stories about when he was in culinary school, and he tried to introduce his friends to jazz, but they couldn't get into it. He felt like me; jazz is a sophisticated acquired level of thinking. When he played the more mellow music such as Coltrane and Miles, I started to slip off to sleep. I must have slept for an hour because when I awakened, he was holding my hand. "Hi, sleepyhead! Bathroom break yet?" he asked.

"Yes, at the next stop if that's okay."

We drove for another fifteen minutes, and then we came across a service station so that he could also get some "petro," as the French called it. Their petro is to our gas. I got out and went to get the key to the bathroom. I hated pissing out in public, period, because you never knew the condition of the bathrooms. However, I was pleasantly surprised the bathroom—or the "chiottes," colloquially speaking, as the French called it—was in pretty good condition. I got some jelly beans for the road because I liked them and hoped he liked them as well. I pulled out my bag, and he said he'd take the red ones.

Forty-five minutes later, I saw a sign that said Monaco. My eyes lit up. "Are you kidding me? Monaco is where Josephine Baker is buried!" I shouted. "I have to go to her gravesite tomorrow."

"Okay, we will," he committed.

We pulled up at this cottage hotel name La Maison Bleue. We got out, and I reminded him I didn't bring any extra clothes, but luckily, I always kept a toothbrush in my purse. He said to me, "Then I hope I thought of everything," and smiled. It was surreal. I was so happy. We checked in separate rooms under his name. I went up to my room and inspected the room's view and the bathroom. It was a traditional stone-built hotel with lovely amenities. Since he was next door to me, our rooms overlooked the patio where people were sitting, eating, and drinking. There was music playing as well. I took a wild leap into the bed into the feathered comforters that enveloped me. I opened the closet, and there, I saw clothes, jeans, jackets, shirts, and blouses. There were already toothbrushes in the bathroom with the niceties that came along with a five-star hotel. I was so impressed. Thirty minutes later, he buzzed my room and asked if I was ready to enjoy the night. I met him outside my door, and as we walked to the elevator, he asked me if he did okay with the clothes. And I said yes, "Wow, you nailed it!"

We were about thirty minutes from Monaco, but in between, there was this quaint little town called Haut Var, where there were cobblestone streets and lots of hills. That's where we headed. We parked and walked the narrow streets looking into the homes of the residents. They seemed unfretted by the tourist looking into their homes. I noticed each home had these beads that hung loosely from their doors. Strangely enough, you could hear the sounds of the beads as you walked the streets. I mentioned that to George, and he said he would have been disappointed had I not noticed that because that was what the town was famous for—the sounds of the beads. When you reached the bottom of the street and looked back, you could see a prism of beads flying and sounding almost like a well-tuned symphony. It was unbelievable.

We went into a local pub that was quiet but had a presence. We sat and talked with the locals for a while. I was feeling giddy and had passed my three-drink limit but felt nothing. I was sipping French wine. Around midnight, it was time to get up to go to our next destination. When I stood up, I was stepping pretty high as I walked. If you've ever been tipsy, you know how difficult it was to focus on a straight walk. I stopped and looked at George who saw in my eyes that I needed some air. He put his arms around my waist and guided me to the door and up the cobblestone street. He told me he had another surprise for me. We walked to the car, and I started feeling better. I drank the Pellegrino I brought with me from the pub. He took me to this small cottage, and we got out. When we entered, it there was a large fireplace. The strangest thing was this fireplace was embedded into a tree trunk with limbs that were raised through the roof, and you could see the stars. In the middle of the floor was a lion's claw tub with tall fixtures where the water would run on both ends of the tub. The toilet itself was a separate area in the corner with a closed door. In front of the tub was the largest furry white rug I had ever seen in my life. In the opposite far corner, there was a tall bed, so tall it had steps to climb into it. The cottage had wooden floors. There was a kitchenette that protruded out from the cottage in a sort of cul-de-sac. A wine rack wall stood near the entrance of the kitchenette. Next to that was an old record player, but it had a CD player as well. There was no TV; nothing but nature at its best.

I turned to George and asked, "Who the fuck lives here?"

He laughed so hard he bent over to laugh. He looked at me as he took my shawl and said, "We do for tonight if you want to, or we can go back to the hotel. You tell me what you want, and I'll do it."

I turned to him and, without hesitation, said, "Okay, we're here tonight!"

The fire was just magnificent. Right after that, it started to rain. At that moment, I witnessed the most beautiful thing. When the rain cascaded from the top of that gigantic tree, it would drizzle down into a stoned throttle that was built into the floor, so not only did you hear the rain falling, you could also hear its constant flow after falling. George walked over to the record player and pulled out his CD case. He played Etta James's "Again." I lay on my back on the rug and listened to the lyrics. I asked him if that was his favorite, and he said yes. We both smiled because we agreed we had old souls.

The lyrics were so beautiful and profound:

Again
This couldn't happen again
This is that once in a lifetime
This is the thrill divine

What's more
This never happened before
Though I have prayed for a lifetime
That such as you would suddenly, suddenly be mine

Mine to hold as I'm holding you now
And never, never, never so near
Mine to have when the now
And the here disappear

What matters, what matters, dear, for when
This doesn't happen again
We'll have this moment forever
But never, never again

Mine to hold as I'm holding you now
And never, never, never so near
Mine to have when the now
And the here disappear and oh

What matters, what matters, what matters, dear, for when
This doesn't happen again
We'll have this moment forever
But never, never again, again
Never, never again, again

He poured each of us a glass of wine. We toasted to the night and to the time we would spend together. I took my sandals off and he his shoes. I lay in one direction, and he lay beside me in the opposite direction, holding hands in silence. He got up to get another bottle of wine, and as he walked, I told him about Michael Franks. He wasn't familiar but was anxious to hear his music. When he returned, he knelt down to pour another glass. He paused and put the bottle down and then laid in the same direction as me. He told me how much he had been thinking about me for all the years we were apart. He said he had dated other women, and he had some nice relationships, but they did not compare to the genuine, sweet, and opinionated person I was. I shared that I had thought about him as well; I had attempted some relationships that didn't turn out to be what I thought they should have been, and so I walked away.

He leaned over and asked if he could kiss me, and I whispered yes. He kissed me so slowly and passionately; first, my forehead and then my ears, my neck, my eyeslids, and finally his lips touched mine. I couldn't attempt to articulate what that moment felt like. His lips brushed mine softly, delicately, like a butterfly's wings, just long enough that I could inhale my breath, feel the warmth of his skin, and smell him. He placed my hands, locked in his above my head, and kissed me passionately. I grabbed his face and pulled him close to me. I've never tasted anything quite like that kiss. I thought right then about the moment we were sharing, when time paused and all my wildest dreams felt possible. I got up and went to the tub. I turned on the water and added the lavender bubble bath. It was perfect for that moment. While I let the water run, I pulled off my dress. I watched him watching me with his wanting eyes. I peeled off my underwear and stood there. I got in the tub. He walked over to the tub and washed my back while putting the glass of wine to my lips. Total quietness. I swallowed the wine, and then he kissed me again. There were no words at all. There was a natural flow to everything that happened. He got up and took his clothes off while watching me. He climbed in the tub with me. I placed my right leg on his right shoulder. Still, no words spoken. He began to rub my feet, then my legs. Then he started to kiss my legs. He pulled both my legs to his shoulders and kissed them passionately. He lifted out of the tub and walked over to get a towel. I stood up, and he wrapped me meticulously in the towel and lifted me up in his arms. He carried me over to the bed and laid me on the bed with the towel on. He asked me if I wanted more wine. I said no. He walked over to get something out of his jacket pocket and came back and then over to the CD player. He played Donnie Hathaway's "For All We Know" appropriately. He sat on the bed and then started back kissing me again. It started as a tickle and a flutter in my stomach and built into a warm pressure; he spread my legs, kissing me first, then my breast so gently. When he kissed my stomach, I shivered uncontrollably with pleasure, not pain. He placed his mouth on my vagina very slowly. He spent twenty minutes just pleasing me, making me feel good, and I've never felt so pampered in my life.

Finally, my first and great orgasm happened. It paralyzed me for a minute. He kissed my legs, which were still trembling, and worked his way back to me. I whispered I hadn't been intimate with a man like I knew he wanted to be with me at that moment. He said he would honor that; he would be gentle, and he wouldn't do anything I didn't want to do. He asked me to relax, and I did. I'm talking my eyes were closed, but I could see and feel colors radiating out of me. It was super. When he put his penis around the entrance of my vagina, I trembled with anticipation. Then I felt him try to enter me once; he checked to see if I was okay, and I murmured yes. It hurt, and he tried slowly again. This time, pain met pleasure. His soft rhythmic thrusts in me became easier. I began to feel uninhibited; I relaxed and enjoyed every thrust. I had two more orgasms. After he had taken care of me several times, then he had an orgasm. I could feel him even though he had a rubber on. I felt him explode inside the walls of my vagina. I couldn't discern where my body ended and his began at that moment. He whispered to me, "I want you in my life, Lisa." He held me in his arms all night long into the early morning, and he made love to me again.

Later that morning, we got up, took a bath together, and prepared to depart. On the ride back to our hotel, he finally told me this cottage was a friend of his, and he wanted to share time with me at the cottage. He thanked me for sharing the time together. We arrived back at the hotel, and I went to my room as he went to his for a change of clothing. I slipped into a white silk blouse with jeans and a blue denim jacket, freshened up, and met him downstairs on the hotel patio for breakfast. I felt different. I couldn't explain the feeling of joy and pleasure but most of all happiness I had. When George came down, he gave me a peck on the lips and sat down. "Okay," he said, "you want to go to Josephine Baker's gravesite, and that we will do." He had this map in front of him, looking for the location, and asked me to order for him the same thing I was having.

He found the gravesite, and he looked at me with this great big smile. We'd leave as soon as we finish breakfast. He reached across the table to hold my hand. I finally realized I was sitting across from my best friend and lover now. I expressed how much I enjoyed myself the night before and that I appreciated his tenderness with me for a first timer. He responded by sharing that he wanted to make sure that my first experience having sex was more than just sex. He exclaimed, "I hope you felt how I feel about you. Anyone can have meaningless sex. I wanted you to be with me because you wanted to be with me. That made it so special for me, and I will never forget what we shared last night." I took his hand and kissed it because there was no need to say anything more. We went back up to grab our things out of the room and placed them in the car. We were on our way to Monaco Cemetery. While we were riding, he asked, "Tell me about Josephine Baker."

That wasn't a difficult ask. First and foremost, she was one of Roger's first clients. That spoke volumes. I started telling him about how much I loved her as a person and then her social activism. I wanted him to understand that Josephine Baker had a sadness in her heart because she was not well received and respected by white America, in the country where she was born. They blackballed her, and so she left the country that decided she didn't deserve to be humanized to live in a country that fell in love with her. "Did you know that she worked for the French Resistance during World War II and during the fifties and sixties? She decided to devote herself to fighting segregation and racism in the United States. She started making a comeback to the stage in 1973 but died of a cerebral hemorrhage in 1975. She was buried with military honors. She was the first American-born woman and for sure black woman to receive full French military honors at her funeral. Paris was so respectful of her that on the day of her funeral, even in her death, she locked up the streets of Paris one last time. That's why she was buried at the Cimetière de Monaco in Monte Carlo."

As I talked, he was so quiet. He said to me, "A person our country could have loved too if not for racism."

"Yep," I quipped, "America's loss and France's gain, yes?"

When we finally arrived, we were right on time. They only allowed the public in from 7:00 a.m. to 8:00 p.m.; it was around 9:00 a.m., so there were not many people there. It was a solemn time for me as I stood there and imagined in my mind how Josephine felt because in reality, blacks in America were like Josephine Baker. My Granny had always reminded me of what our country was about and how it fought tooth and nail to keep people like myself from participating not in the American dream but in our own dreams. After the grave visit, we walked around the piers in Monaco and decided it was time to leave. On the ride back, George held my hand all the way, and I moved over to lay my head on his shoulder to sleep the rest of he way. When we arrived at Roger's place, he walked me to the coach cottage. We talked, and we both agreed we had something special, and we could not allow the world to drive us apart. I told him yes, and the closer we got to falling in love; and the more deeply in love we became, we could anticipate that we were going to have a bumpy road ahead.

New Beginnings

I STOOD WITH my back against the door when George walked away. I knew for sure we had something special, and I wanted it to last. I packed my things and walked over to the cottage to thank Roger and his lovely wife for hosting me at their cottage. Roger was such a gentleman; he asked me if I could leave the sketches of the shoes I had shared with staff with him to peruse. "Of course," I said. I handed them to him, and by that time, the van had arrived to transport me to the train station. I got four pecks on the cheeks, two on each.

Sitting on the train, I started replaying in my mind the week I had in Provence. I wanted to remember every moment. I wanted to bottle my experience in Haut Var with George. Before he departed, we agreed to talk once or twice a week and to visit each other at least once a month or more if possible. He and I realized how important it was for us to work on our careers; it was an integral part of our happiness because we liked what we did. We both were invested into our careers.

When I arrived in Paris, I hopped in a taxi to the apartment. I almost crawled up the steps because I was tired. I opened my door and stood in the window gazing at the glinting lights on the Eiffel

Tower. Finally, I unpacked and laid across the bed. As I unpacked, I found a note on the hotel's letterhead from George: "My darling Lisa, we have finally found each other again. We can never lose each other, never. Yours always, George."

An hour later, the phone rang. It was George checking to see if I had arrived safely. We talked for about thirty minutes and ended it because he had to work at the restaurant that evening. We promised never to hold on to anger, never hang up angry, and never go to bed angry with each other about anything, and I could live with that. I called my Granny, and she was so happy to hear from me. I told her I had a boyfriend. She started screaming on the phone. "Oh, LiLi, I am so happy for you. Are you happy?" she replied.

"Yes, ma'am, I am. I need to tell you that he is white, Granny," I confessed.

"Well, LiLi, your heart doesn't put color or race to matters of love. I just want you to be happy, darling. To have found someone you entrust your heart to is a big step for you, I know. I also know you don't trust easily, so this person must be special."

"He is, Granny. It's George, you know, the boy I met when Pops was working at the lieutenant governor's house. We were writing letters to each other and lost contact for a while, but I saw him in Provence while on a retreat."

She said, "That is a good sign that you were able to find each other again."

I noticed Granny's voice sounded tired, and I inquired about it. She said she had been getting tired lately and kept getting colds. She had not gone to the doctor yet. I reprimanded her and told her to get to the doctor. "Granny, I won't be at peace until I know you're all right," I swore.

She promised she would. I said my goodbye and then called my dad to make sure he was aware Granny wasn't feeling well. I asked Pops to make a visit and take her to the doctor; he said he would, and that gave me a level of confidence. I felt a great deal of comfort that my Granny was not shaken by the fact that George was white. However, I knew I would have to inevitably share the news with my Pops as well. I thought what irony my Pops had spent many years on the shortcutting his walk through the Capitol to the lieutenant governor's office on business. He often shared with us how painful it felt to look up every time during that walk to see a Confederate flag flapping in the wind because he hated what that flag represented. Then he would curse and say, "Those peckerwoods would still have us as slaves if they could and if we allowed it." My Pops was a staunch supporter of the NAACP. He was a card-carrying member and did so unapologetically. I understood why he felt that way not only because we were black, but also he knew so many sides of white folks because they were his clients. He'd seen and heard the worse of them and the best of them as well.

George and I would keep our commitment to call and visit each other over the next three weeks. I called him to let him know I would be crazy busy preparing for fashion week and that I would call as soon as I got an opportunity. "No problem, my love, I get it. We both are pretty busy." He explained that the restaurant owners in Provence and the one in Lyon were pushing to become Michelin-star restaurants. I listened attentively. He told me, "In order to earn one star, a restaurant had to be considered 'a very good restaurant in its category.' For two stars, the requirement was 'excellent cooking, worth a detour.' To qualify for the elusive three stars, a restaurant must serve up 'exceptional cuisine, worth a special journey.'" He really felt the pressure because the top chef had brought on two new sous chefs to work with them in accomplishing the goals the owners had set. I reassured him that I supported him all the way.

Three weeks before fashion week, Roger and his wife Andree agreed amicably to a divorce. I didn't see that coming, but I was sure they wanted what was best for both. It saddened me a little because I had become fond of her. Also, they had been together for some time, and I couldn't imagine what might have been the cause for the divorce. Later on, she would pop into the fashion house occasionally, and they would talk and laugh together. It made the entire house feel comfortable because we really loved Andree. She was a talking machine that if you listened carefully, she had some serious shit to share that you could learn from.

It was September 1984, and preparation for fashion week in Paris was in full swing. Roger made us aware when he hired us that he was looking for fresh ideas, and that's why he had brought us on to renew the exquisiteness of the Viveront shoe. His shoes were always an experience and known around the world as the premier shoe to have in your closet. You are talking about a man that understood women so much that he could change a "whore shoe" to a respectable shoe for women all over the world. He was the creator of the stiletto, and women loved him for it. Roger had a great eye for shoes and an exceptional understanding of women, their feet, and their legs. He just knew what looked great on not just a stylish woman but also women who might be made by the shoe. His shoes had pearls, diamonds, and always something intriguing that usually made the "cocktail party's thing to discuss" list. Shoes had been worn by queens and those who would be queens.

We had other designer partners especially during fashion week. The whole positioning and setups in preparation for fashion week was a learning experience. Selecting models, designing sets, and working with people across the spectrum of fashion. Thousands would preorder shoes before fashion week even started. People came to fashion week from all walks of life. Business, entertainment, movie, and film industry—they all came to see and to be seen as well. All the fashion houses were jumping. There were parties to attend and some to avoid. I had to get the scoop on which was which. Roger was getting up in age, but it did not interfere with his competence in the industry. He loved working and collaborating with other famous designers as well. But they loved calling on him because they knew he had established himself in the market as a premier designer and businessman as well. My first fashion week was a quick and sometimes arduous undertaking, but I got through it; we all got through it. I even discovered it could bring some to their senses as well. One night after a show, we were so exhausted Andrea and Pete were engaging me in a conversation and Andrea even leaned on my shoulder with her head as she was so tired. I was reciprocal. I laughed and cursed with them that night as well.

Roger gave us the next week off but not until we had processed the orders. Whew! So many lessons were learned during fashion week. During fashion week, I met a businessman that was known for financing promising fashion designers. His name was Jean Claude. People spoke very favorably of him. I struck up a chat with him at an after-party, and he appeared to be very knowledgeable of the business and genuinely interested in the industry. I took his card, wrote a note on the back of the card, and the following week committed to giving him a call. I made the call to see if we could do lunch. He suggested the place and time, and what could I say, I took a leap of faith. I checked my bank account because I didn't really know where he might suggest for lunch. Like my Pops always said, if you invite someone to lunch, you pick up the check. I thought it couldn't be over a thousand dollars, and if so, I was fucked. I knew it would be unethical to use the credit card Roger had given us, so I needed to have my shit together; this was a personal thing, not a Roger thing. In the meantime, I took time to work on my portfolio, not the shoe portfolio but the menswear portfolio I'd been laboring on for months. There were two more days before the lunch, and I had the entire week off, so I called Patek to invite her out for dinner.

Patek and I met in the lobby of the apartment building and hopped in a taxi to the Latin Quarters. She selected a fabulous restaurant where we had eaten many times, L'arbre A Cannelle. It was the perfect place for us to chat and bring each other up to date. Patek was so happy because she had spent some time alone with her boyfriend totally isolated from his mom and family. "He's such a different person when I am alone with him, but oh God, when we are around his family, he is pensive and on guard," she confessed.

In a humorous way, I shared, "Listen, Patek, he has got to get some balls."

"You're right because he can't even fuck right when we are alone around his parents. It screws with his mind, so he literally needs to get some balls, you know?"

We both laughed as we walked into the restaurant. We asked for a table near the window so that we could people-watch. We both did that a lot. I could qualify gazing because I somewhat was a fashion forecaster; however, I knew good and damn well my people-watching was so that I could find something funny and unique to talk about. Shit, call a spade a spade, as my brother used to say. Patek's reason was that it gave her inspiration. Right. We ordered a nice French wine, a cheese course, bread, and our entrée. Parisians are insulted if you eat less than two hours, so it worked well for us to catch up on things.

"What's been going on with you?" Patek asked.

"Well, where should I start?"

"Ah hell, some shit has gone down." Patek sighed.

I should've been the happiest person in the world right now, but I couldn't release the thing in the back of my mind about Jules. I talked about the incident that happened with Jules in detail again. She was so stunned the first time I told her and almost speechless. Patek reached across the table for my hands and showed compassion. She asked me if I was okay and, in the same breath, told me to never carry that kind of burden, that I could always feel safe sharing with her. "I just was embarrassed, and I was a little hurt too. Obviously that incident affected me more than I imagined. Even though I had not invested a lot of time or emotions into the relationship, whatever I had invested was crushed," I admitted.

"What a motherfucker!" cited Patek.

"There it is," I said, laughing at Patek's facial expression.

"Lisa, I had a gay friend that used to always tell me when I had a date, make sure you are going out with a man, miss thang! I used to say stop, but I saw what he meant."

I told her I just kept myself busy because that was important. In reality, the most embarrassing thing was when I went home, my brothers were teasing me about a boyfriend, and they never knew I was sitting there tormented by what I had experienced. "But I do have some better news."

"Come on with it," Patek snapped.

"Remember we had the retreat for a week in Provence, yes?"

"Right," Patek nodded.

I told her I saw George and how it all happened at the restaurant. "Shut the fuck up."

"Yep, I saw him. He's a chef at the restaurant there. We spent some time together." Patek kept digging. "Okay, we spent a night together in a small villa ten minutes outside of Monaco called Haut Var. He was so sweet. He planned the entire time we were together." I told her about the cottage where we spent overnight, and then I finally shared we slept together. She screamed so loud people in the restaurant turned to see if she was okay. I gestured to her to pipe it down.

"How was your first time?" she inquired.

I told her I had allowed Jules to perform oral sex on me but not penetrate, and I felt violated after I found him with that guy. But I also conveyed that my experience with George was way beyond what I could have imagined. "He was so gentle and caring. His every move was to please me, and he did it tenderly, Patek. At first, it hurt, but because he was so tender, he was careful, and he made sure I knew he wanted to please me and that I was okay."

She asked, "Is that the only reason it hurt, my dear?"

I blushed and said no.

"That's what I'm talking about. I am so glad you had that experience, Lisa. You deserved him," Patek confirmed. We toasted to my officially becoming a woman.

The rest of the evening, we talked about business. I made her aware that I was going to be meeting with this guy named Jean Claude, a fashion financier. "I'm going to try and start my own fashion house in a year, Patek, and I need the funding."

"That sounds great, Lisa. I wish I could find someone that would do the same for me. I have to depend upon my parents and the sale of my paintings, which don't give me the type of seed money I need for my own gallery and place to paint. Keep me posted on that, and I will keep my fingers crossed for you, sweetie!" Patek affirmed. We enjoyed the remainder of our dinner.

At the retreat, I discovered running a fashion house was going to be expensive, just as Paul told me. The first thing I needed to focus on and have financed was designing and finding private customers to wear them. Once I accrued a certain number, then I could talk about financing a house to design and show. I knew I had to research to see what type of business plan I needed, but I was going to take one step at a time, yes? I spent the next two days researching. I had to go to the library and spend some serious time in there researching the industry so that I could have decent conversation with Jean Claude. I didn't quite trust him enough to tell him my business concept, but I thought I could give him just enough to let him know I was knowledgeable of the business I wanted to pursue.

The next day, I had to meet Jean Claude at Le Bon Georges. I called Patek to inquire about the restaurant once he shared where we would meet, and she was familiar. She said it was a neobistro that combined the flavors of traditional French food with contemporary minimalism and freshness that meant smaller portions with lots of vegetables. Perfect! I met Jean Claude at the restaurant, and I got there ahead of time to demonstrate I believed in punctuality. He was very gracious. We sat, and he ordered a wine-and-cheese course. Our conversation started out with a get-to-know-you type of vibe. That was a great icebreaker. I told him just enough for him to determine my compassion for what I wanted to do. He told me about himself as well. Jean Claude came from what we call in America old money and deep pockets. His parents owned vineyards in the south of France. He only moved to Paris fifteen years ago, but he always had a love for art and fashion. He knew he did not want to be in the wine business, but he also knew he had to find something to convince his parents he was serious about his passion, supporting both industries as a financier. He decided to invest his money in both industries, and it made him profitable and well-known.

I showed him my sketches, and he asked a series of questions about why I was so passionate about what I was doing. I explained it well because he sat and listened attentively. I did tell him in two years I would be ready to launch my own business. I needed to know from him what would satisfy his willingness to invest in me as a businessperson. He said five things: great concept, new and innovative and sustainable, could be profitable, and he felt I had ability to run the business with integrity. I said to him, "That's fair." I told him I was working on a concept, and I would like to come back to him within a year to present my idea for funding.

He said something very interesting to me, "You know, often I meet with people, and they come right at me with a hard sell. Not you. I like that you wanted to know my thoughts and to find about what was important to me as well. I respect that."

"That's critical to the success of the business. I see that all the time from Roger, and that's why people respect him," I responded.

Jean Claude agreed and said I had a great mentor in Roger. We chatted about Paris and how much I liked it, and we chatted about art as well. We spent about two hours of time together, and it ended with me shaking his hand and thanking him for meeting with me. Before he left, he said to me, "See you in a year, yes?"

I smiled and said, "Yes, you will."

We walked in different directions as I waved goodbye to him. Since I was in the Quarters, I decided to walk around a little. I came across a music store and went in to browse. I bought three CDs: two Michael Franks and one Nancy Wilson CD. Not far from there was a postal service, so I packaged and mailed one of the Michael Franks to George and then made my way back home.

In Touch with Myself

I WOKE UP Monday morning feeling rejuvenated. I really had a sense of purpose after speaking with Jean Claude. When I walked in the shop, Roger happened to be in that day. I was earlier than usual that day. I just wanted to settle in and start early. I had that type of energy going for myself. Roger called me into his office space. We laughed and talked for a bit, and then he told me he had spoken with Jean Claude. I was skeptical at first until he said, "I want you to become successful, Lisa. You have a great eye and talent with potential to become a great designer. Let me know when you're ready to take your quantum leap, and I will do what I can for you, okay?"

I paused, and then I was reciprocal. "Roger, you are a great mentor, and I have a lot of respect for you. You have shown me the true meaning of work ethics and how important it is to have passion in what you do. I thank you so much for that. Thank you for offering to help me. I won't forget it." I shook his hand on that and then asked him what's the priority for the day. He showed me some designs he had and asked my opinion of how I could modernize them. The rest of the day went well.

When I reached home, I had mail in my box. It was a letter from George. We agreed to continue to write each other. We had just gotten used to our letters; it created so much anticipation for us both. I waited until I was in my apartment to read it. He had received my CD in the mail, and he had been playing it. He loved it! I knew he would. He had been working pretty steadily because winter was settling in and tourism was not going to be the same in the off season. He wanted to know if that weekend would be good for a visit to Paris. I was so excited. I called him immediately. "Hey, you," I snickered.

"Hi, sweetheart," he said. "I just read your letter, and yes, this weekend would be perfect." He was happy that I said yes. He'd catch the 2:00 p.m. train and would arrive around 5:30 p.m. Friday.

The remainder of the week was very busy. During the days, I worked hard for Roger, and evenings, I worked smart for me. I was intent on starting my own business. Now that I knew Jean Claude was amenable, I needed only to work on plans and product. I visited some of the local fashion schools to talk with students and some instructors just to see what the possibilities might be if I were to use some of them in my business. I was pleasantly surprised the students were pretty committed to the art of fashion, always thinking of something innovative and, as they called it, fresh. By Thursday, I was really tired. I called Patek to see if she and her boyfriend would be available for dinner and jazz Saturday night. Unfortunately, Patek would be in Milan that weekend, so that was a no. I could say I wasn't too disappointed because I loved having him all to myself. I went out to pick up bottles of wine, cheese, and bread. I bought candles, and I made sure my apartment was extra clean. I asked Latecia to recommend restaurants and jazz clubs for the weekend, and she gave me a list to follow up on that evening.

I found what I thought was great. I thought the *Bateaux Parisiens on the Seine River* was a good choice because it had gourmet food, and it was on the Seine. Also, the dating gods smiled on me because I was able to score two front row tickets to *Grande Halle de la Villette;* this was going to be a great surprise for George. *The Grande Halle* was very well-known for its architectural flare. It was located in the old industrial district of Paris. It was made of cast iron and glass. Patek said I would not be disappointed. She raved about the sound;

she said the speakers hung from hooks on the overhead canopy even though they were not easy to see. It had a glass roof, so you could see the stars during the concert. I was looking forward to Saturday. I thought Paris in itself was enough for the first night we would be together. You know, walking around Paris, and let's face it; I had the best seat in the house, as I could see the Eiffel Tower out my huge bay windows. Before going home, I dropped by the electronic store and bought a CD player because I had mostly albums and an old record player for which I loved. Friday morning, I got up spirited and dressed for work. On my way, I decided to drop by the market to pick up a salad for lunch. While browsing, someone came up behind me and placed their hands over my eyes. I didn't quite know what to say. "Okay, you want to tell me who, or do I have to guess?" I uttered. When they took their hands off, I turned to see it was Jules. Honestly, I couldn't even fake a smile. I just looked at him.

"Hi, Lisa," he said.

I responded, "Hi, Jules."

There were a few seconds of silence, then he asked, "How are you are doing?"

I started walking toward the checkout counter as I replied, "I'm doing well, Jules, and you?"

He started telling me the business has been doing well, that he had made a partner.

"Well, good for you, Jules. You always wanted to be a partner, congratulations! Look, I don't want to be rude, but I am trying to make a meeting. It was good to see that you are doing well, bye-bye." I gave a halfway smile and waved goodbye. I didn't look back. It almost fucked with my head, but I would not allow it. I felt sorry for him and almost threw up when I discovered it was his hands on my face. I had closed a chapter in my life.

I hopped in a taxi and burst out of it once it stopped in front of the shop to get to the bathroom before anyone else would come in. It seemed Roger was already there in his office. I ran into the bathroom, washed my face, and put warm compresses on it. When I exited the bathroom, I saw Roger across the room. "Hi, Lisa, his fragile voice said. "I'm on my way to Toulouse today. I'll see you Friday of next week."

"Anything pressing I should follow up on, Roger?" I asked.

"No, we're good, Lisa. Enjoy your weekend," he said as he walked slowly out the door. Roger had to be around eighty years old, but he had the spirit of a twenty-year-old working endlessly and committed to his craft of art. I admired that about him. I never heard him complain. He was always thinking progressively about the possibilities, not the obstacles. I couldn't have had a better mentor.

The day went well. Everyone was on all cylinders after fashion week. We all took an early lunch so that we could leave early. I left the office around 3:30 p.m., which gave me plenty of time to get to the apartment and prepare to greet George. When I arrived, I saw Mete in the lobby. "Mete, comment ça va?"

In his cute little way, he would smile and say, "Je vais bien et vous?"

I started up the stairs and into the apartment. It had begun to rain, and when I got to the apartment, I could see that the fog mystified the Eiffel Tower even more because you could see it engulfed in the fog but piercing through the top. I bathed, lit some candles, put a new CD on, and put a bottle of wine in the fridge to chill before George arrived. The doorman buzzed me to let me know I had a guest. "Have him walk up, please," I said. I heard the knock at the door and rushed to open it. When I opened it, I was so happy to see that beautiful smile on his face. I received kisses on both cheeks and a lengthy embrace, and oh my God, he spelled so damn good. "Hey, you, come on in!" He walked in and stood in the window, taking in the view. "How was your train ride?" I inquired.

"It was okay, lots of families on. That means there were probably more kids than I would have liked for a Friday, but hey, what can you say?"

"Okay. I'll run a bath for you, yes?"

"Thanks, sweetie, I would love that."

I laid the towel and toiletries on the vanity. I had him put his things down and just sit while I ran the bath. I handed him a glass of wine and got a sweet kiss on the lips as a thank-you. While running the bath, I told him to relax and take his time; we're in for the night until Mother Nature cooperated. While he was taking his bath, I sat the small table in front of the window and placed the candles, cheese, bread, and apples on the board and the bottle of wine. He came out of the bedroom dressed and relaxed. He sat for a moment just staring at me, and I had to ask, "What?" He smiled and said he was happy to be with me. I smiled and reached over for a kiss.

We decided when we visited each other that we would do shop-talk for the first hour, and after that (unless dire emergency), time would be devoted to us spending quality time with each other. So I struck up the conversation. "How was your week?" He told me he had a great week, and he felt they would probably get a Michelin star. "Okay, but you don't sound enthusiastic about it!"

"You're right, sweetie, I think it's time for me to strike out on my own."

"Wow, that's great, babe. Tell me more," I insisted. He said he had been working on a plan for the last four years, but he knew he would have to have investors. He felt as a new restaurateur, the only people he could really trust as investors were his family members. He believed if they invested and the first five years didn't meet the goal, he'd have a better chance of working out a compromise with them versus outsiders. I asked, "Are you reluctant to ask your family?"

"I have some reservations because it's family. I would have to have some real understanding between us about what the invest-ments mean, as it relates to me because that's important to me," he vehemently said.

I told him it sounded fair to me. "Darling, I'm here for you, and I know you're going to be successful because you've always had the passion for what you do." I confirmed he should take the leap of faith.

He told me what that meant was that he would have to quit the current job after December or at the beginning of next year and spend a month or so in the States to try and convince his family to invest in his business. "So I suppose becoming a Michelin-star recip-ient would be proof of power, yes?" I quipped.

"You're right, and I have confidence we will do well on that. Enough about me. What's going on with you, sweetie?" he inquired.

"Well, I am thinking I want to launch my own business as well in the next year or two. I want to start small by doing personal couture. That means I would need to secure a nice list of clients."

"Oh, I can see you doing that," he acquiesced.

"My target market would be men only because very few women are doing that. You've never seen any of my sketches, have you?"

He drank some wine and said with glee, "No, do you mind sharing?"

I went to my drawing table to pull my portfolio. I watched him as he looked page for page; his eyes would light up with pleasure. "Sweetie, I didn't realize you were so talented. These are impressive." I told him I met with Jean Claude who had expressed interest in investing. To let him know I had done my homework, I told him I had researched Jean Claude and the probability of the business as well and said, "I think if I follow the road plan, I should be okay. I got Roger's blessings as well."

"Well, looks as though you have put some thought into it, and I am here for you as well, darling. So let's toast to our success." We did and sealed it with a passionate kiss.

"Looks like the rain has stopped. Let's get out of here for an hour." I got up, and so did he. I grabbed my jacket, and so did he. We walked down the steps, and at the bottom of the steps I saw Mete. He looked at me and winked with a smile. I insisted, "Mete, permettez-moi de vous présenter mon petit ami," let me introduce you to my boyfriend, "George. George, cette Mete."

"Bon jour," said George and shook his hand. It was important for me to introduce George because Mete had never seen a man come out of my apartment. Introducing him to George meant both George and he were special to me.

As we went outside the apartment, we decided to walk. We simultaneously reached for each other's hands. We were walking the streets of Paris in the misty breeze. We sat on a park bench and listened to the trees. Cool breezes rustled its green leaves and acorns. The sun in its final hour peeked through wind-blown gaps, creating dancing glimmers of light in the shade below the tree canopy, but beneath the tree, we sat holding hands and kissing to show our approval of what we witnessed. On the way back, we stopped at a pretzel street food cart and shared a pretzel. Time moved fast, and we wanted it to stop just for us. We watched other couples express their affections to our amusement. We made our way near the Eiffel Tower as it perfectly timed itself to glisten with lights twinkling like stars. We turned to each other and laughed because we succinctly thought about the gravitas of that moment. It started to rain, and I mean pouring; so we decided to run the blocks to the apartment. He was guiding me through the rain as we splattered in the rain, laughing and cursing all the way. When we arrived, we were drenched in water, but we didn't mind. I grabbed towels from the linen closet for us to dry with.

We peeled out of our clothing and wrapped ourselves in the towels. I lit the candles and walked over to the record player. He walked to the cooler to get another bottle of wine. He walked over where I stood. I chose the album while he touched my back. I leaned forward and put the album on, Nancy Wilson's "The Very Thought of You." It was the perfect tune for the moment. He gave me my glass of wine, and we both walked to the window to toast to the Eiffel Tower for obliging us the view we both so enjoyed at that moment. We danced together for the duration of the song. I sat on the end of bed with criss-crossed legs and let the towel drop. He went to the kitchen and came back with another bottle. When he let his towel drop, my heart fluttered as I brought him close to me. I touched him so gently and told him what I wanted to do but warned him this was my first time. I took him in my hand and guided his penis to my mouth. I enjoyed knowing I was pleasing him so much. I started slowly, as I wanted to take my time and enjoy the moment. I knew this was as private and intimate as it got, but I wanted to make it special for him and for me.

His wanting eyes showed me how much he enjoyed it; when he swelled in my mouth, I stopped. I lifted on my knees and kissed his lips purposefully. He whispered to me, "Baby, that was unbelievable, thank you." I pulled the covers back and laid my head on the pillows.

He entered the bed and pulled me all the way to his mouth. He made love to me with his tongue, and it made me tremble with excitement. Every time I would express my feelings, he would go deeper. So sweet yet so sacred this moment was. I had an orgasm, and my body shook with pleasure. He put my legs down, and he came to lie beside me; we spooned for about thirty minutes. Both our hearts were beating fast. He turned to me and looked straight into my eyes. I turned on my back, and he mounted me. When he entered me, the proverbial floodgates opened. He would ask "Do you like this? Do you want to do this?" before trying anything, which was totally not the consent norm of the time and which, as a feminist myself, I found very sexy and reassuring. We looked at each other so intensely and had an orgasm at the same time. We turned to face each other, and he said to me, "Lisa, I love you."

My eyes teared up as I responded, "George, I love you."

We kissed and fell asleep.

The next day, we had a great morning. He prepared breakfast and served me in bed. We got up and bathed, got dressed, and hit the Quarters. George wanted to take a look at some of the cuisine. We also visited Sacré-Cœur, the *Basilica of the Sacred Heart of Paris*. I supposed I needed to light two candles and ask for forgiveness because I had a lot to be forgiven after last night. Returning home in good time before the evening was great. We were able to get at least three hours of sleep. We dressed and headed to the *Bateaux Parisiens on the Seine River*. We sat at the window looking out at the Seine. It was a romantic evening at best. George and I talked about his trip back home in January. He would probably be there from January to March, or three months. I loved that he wanted me to feel okay with that. I explained that we had to make Christmas and New Year's Day in Paris very special. He looked at me and smiled.

We left the restaurant and headed to my big surprise for him. Our taxi let us off in front of the *Grande Halle de la Villette*. When we entered the building, George couldn't help but notice the architecture. He was amazed, but not as amazed as when he got the program bill to see who was performing. When he read it, he looked over at me with his huge smile, and he kissed me. "Baby, you have made my night, Miles Davis. Oh my, this is amazing!"

I thought, mission accomplished. This weekend had been everything I wanted it to be, and it hadn't even ended.

Chapter 23

The Death of a Quiet Giant

JANUARY 1985 WAS a busy year, and the month of January was so busy for us at the shop and for me personally as well. Some of the associates were preparing to attend the New York Fashion Week. Although I was given an option, I could not go because I had begun working with male clients on the side for my own business venture. This wasn't anything I would have shared with regular associates, so I told them it was great to give others the experience. I had asked Mete to look out for me, as I was looking for a space nearby to set up a small studio for my business. I found out from Mete that the flat below me was up for leasing; and I thought it would be great to lease it as well because of the great rate. The fact that it was in proximity and I could make it into a great personal couture space was just what I needed. I knew there would not be a lot of foot traffic because it was by appointment only. That proved to be a smart move. I set it up where it looked like a personalized space for men's couture. In the back bedroom housed my product and doubled as a sewing room as well. A client could see me by appointment; only meaning it was the luxury and exclusivity they were paying for. I hired a student from API Parsons of Paris to intern, working the phone and setting appointments, and I gave him a stipend for the four hours a week.

During busy times, I would eventually increase his days and stipend as well. My greatest expense was the fabric. I had to order it from Milan. I was fortunate because Amanda hooked me up with a guy that owned a factory, and he gave me a break. I was on a tight budget. Every dollar I made from working with Roger and doing some special events on the side, I invested it back into the business.

After six months, or in June, I decided it was time to go back to Jean Claude so that he could make good on the investment. I set up an appointment with him to go over where I was with my venture and to talk about inventory and start-up costs. We met at a local bistro and hammered out the details. He was pleasantly surprised and pleased with what I had done so far. He told me he would have his assistant call me and make arrangements to transfer the funds to my business account as soon as I signed the contract. When I left the meeting, I was on an adrenaline high! I called George, who was now in the States, to share the good news. He was so happy for me. He had just left for the States a week before my meeting with Jean Claude. He mentioned he was spending time with his family, and he would give them a couple of weeks before he started discussing investments with them.

The following week on a Saturday, I received a call from Jean Claude's assistant to tell me the amount of the investment and that he would be sending over the agreement by courier. Within three hours, the courier was at my place with the agreement. I looked it over and called Patek to see if her friend who was a corporate attorney could eyeball it for me. Patek set up dinner with her friend to introduce us and to have her look over the contract.

After work that Monday, as exhausted as I was, I traveled to meet with Patek and her friend Anatasie. When I arrived, both were already there. Anatasie was very intelligent and was a great supporter of women in business. She was a short but cute woman, pretty much straight to the point. She wanted to know about me first, and I shared with her what my vision was over a bottle or two of wine. Patek had done a great job as my friend telling Anatasie about me because as I was talking, she would acquiesce by saying, "Patek told me…" She looked the agreement over and felt it was fair. She also thought the return on the investment or ROI was the key to the agreement. She said I should be able to pay the investor off within a year if I continued the rate of business I was doing. She asked me to explain how the business worked. I explained the business was a two-person operation for right now. The idea was to give exclusive service to men in customizing their suits. My clients were by invitation only, but what that meant was that I would definitely have to accrue an A list of clients to sustain the business. My goal should be to pay out the investor within a year and a half. I was very impressed with Anatasie and asked how much I owed her. She said nothing, but she would like to become my attorney going forward. I said, "Wow, I really appreciate it. I would definitely use your services!" We all sat and talked a while. Patek and I left together.

When I got home, I laid flat on the bed, looking to the sky. I said, "God, I don't know why I deserve your gifts, but I hope I can truly earn your grace going forward." Twenty thousand dollars was more than I expected. It would help me jumpstart my business without stretching me out. Jean Claude understood that if I were successful, so would he; he would refer some top-of-the-line clients to me going forward. What changed my business tremendously was when I purchased my first cell phone. The cell phone also allowed me to respond quicker to fussy clients. It also allowed me to talk with my sweetheart at my pleasure as well.

I had been working with Patek, Anatasie, and my student assistants for the last six months to plan a private showing for my clients. I left the meticulous planning to the students and focused my attention on getting the suits ready for the show. We all met to go over the plans two weeks before the date. Patek identified a beautiful loft located at Rue du Buisson Saint Louis. It was perfect for the occasion. Personal invitations went out to twenty-five high-volume clients. I designated securing male models to Latecia. The catering was solidified, and we were good to go. We wanted to host an event with our private clients because more than the product itself, to have a private showing meant something very special. We had the best service for our clientele. When guests entered, we had servers for everything. We would have servers to take wraps, for champagne, and hors d'oeuvres and finally a bartender. I even had a server whose only job was to check the bathroom every fifteen minutes. Some men didn't know how to clean like women. I happened to know that because I had two brothers. You know, the intricate things like drying the vanity and pissing on the floor. Patek thought it would be great to have little take-aways for our guests.

The showing was on the hottest day of June. I was a little worried people would not want to show up in the heat, but they did. The show went well, the guests felt exclusive, and at the end of the night, Jean Claude himself was raving about how much he was impressed. I knew that the real success of this event would be realized in the new or repeat business I would get going forward. That's where my mind was.

Mostly all the guests had left with the exception of maybe two. One guest was more interested in a male model, and so he was hanging around for him. The other was a well-known Parisian businessman. When I finally walked away from the door saying goodbye to guests, I walked back over to the bar for my first drink of the night. Patek was wrapping up an art deal for one of the pieces she showcased that evening. This gentleman, Alexandre by name, walked over to me and started to chat. He talked about the suits in detail. He wanted to know the price points; he talked about the fabrics, so I engaged him for about thirty minutes. Finally, he wanted to set an appointment, so I quickly asked one of the students to look at the calendar and make the appointment at that moment. I expressed to him how I was happy he enjoyed the show and that I looked forward to doing business with him. He gave me one of his business cards (I wrote a note on the back of the card). He took my hand and gave it a smooch. I bade him good night and started helping to rack the clothes. Orchestrating the cleanup of the place, I paid the servers, bartender, and maids for the evening. It was a good night.

Patek and I hopped in a taxi, and before she went upstairs, I gave her an envelope and asked her not to open it until she got to her flat. She called me fifteen minutes later and asked me what the money was for, and I explained the event would not have been successful without her. She kept saying I didn't have to, but I told her,

"Yes, I did because you are my best friend, but I also respect your expertise."

"Thank you, my friend," she said.

We both said good night. I got out of my heels, designed by Roger of course, and rubbed my aching feet because I had been on them all night. It was midnight in Paris but 5:00 p.m. in Chicago where George was visiting. I called him, and he was on his way out to meet his cousins and father to talk about his concept. He took time to hear about my event and then said how proud he was of me and that he loved me. I wished him luck and hung up. I peeled out of my clothes and jumped right into my warm bed.

A week after the show, I received about ten responses from the twentyfive men I'd invited. I felt that was a great ROI. We set appointments for each. One of the key appointments was with Alexandre. His appointment was coming up at 2:00 p.m. I walked downstairs earlier at 1:00 p.m. When he came up, I took his jacket; I offered him tea, wine, coffee, or champagne. He opted for champagne. I took a champagne glass and popped the bottle, poured it, and set the bottle in an ice bucket. I sat with him for a consultation to determine his needs. I showed him fabrics, twills, etc. and made my final recommendation for fabrics. He finally selected what he wanted, and I went over the policies for a custom suit. We wrapped it up by getting the measurements. I did not want to talk while measuring because it was a personal thing getting the measurements in places that were private and could make someone very uncomfortable. As the designer, I couldn't show that discomfort. While I measured him, he was very cooperative. "It's going to be a six to eight weeks turnaround time with two follow-up fittings." He was okay with that. I thanked him but noticed he wanted to finish his champagne, and I thought, *That's fair.* While he sat sipping, he asked me about myself. To keep it professional, I gave him the most basic information possible, mostly about how much I enjoyed working with Roger. I spoke in all generalities and didn't ask him any personal questions. I learned that from Roger. He was very pleasant as I assisted him with putting on his jacket. We shook hands, and I closed the door behind him.

That Monday I received a callback from Alexandre for four suits. He asked me to select the fabrics, and that was huge. "All business suits," he explained. I queried him about colors, and he said navy blue and one brown. This was huge. That meant I would be working twelve-hour days for the next six to eight weeks. Five suits plus the additional ten orders were a great start. Fifteen hundred dollars per suit was not bad at all. I spent the next eight weeks working my ass off. I had students who could sew, working on stitching for me, and we worked way into the mornings. At this juncture, I started thinking about how to manage my time better. I realized it wasn't the time management; it was where I was devoting my time. I had to make a decision. I talked it over with George. I decided I would have to take a leap of faith to go full-time with my business, and I needed to sit with Roger and let him know.

That Sunday evening, I took a long-awaited bath, and my cell phone rang. I jumped out of the tub, almost slipping on the tile floor, and ran to the phone that was stuffed in my purse. "Hello," I said. It was Latecia, but she was crying. I asked her "Latecia, what's wrong? Are you okay?" She said no. She was calling because Roger had passed. My heart sank; I dropped the phone, and I mean I couldn't stop crying. I kept asking what happened, and she told me nothing happened. He died in his sleep. I was so emotionally drained by this news. Roger meant a lot to me. He came from humble beginnings because he was an orphan. He was unassuming but well respected by his peers. He was a quiet storm with the most pronounced work ethic I had ever witnessed. He gave me an opportunity to apprentice under him. He was my mentor and friend. I was saddened and found it difficult to even go back to the office. His companion made a follow-up call to me and asked if I would go into the shop to be there when Latecia shared it with the staff. I owed Roger that and more.

The next day when we got in, Latecia broke the news to staff. We all cried profusely as we hugged one another and cried on shoulders. All day long, there was a silence. The news media started announcing the death, which made it even more difficult. His companion called to let us know that Roger's son would be arriving to take over the business.

That Wednesday we left for Toulouse, France, for Roger's funeral. There were people there from all over the world. It was by invitation only. It was private, a definite tribute to Roger. My heart was heavy because I had lost a friend, a mentor, and someone who believed in me. I went home and read this beautiful poem by Yahuda Halevi that went like this:

'Tis a Fearful Thing

'Tis a fearful thing to love what death
can touch.
A fearful thing to love, to hope, to
dream, to be—to be, And oh, to lose.
A thing for fools, this,
And a holy thing, a holy
thing
to love.
For your life has lived in me, your
laugh once lifted me, your word was
gift to me.
To remember this brings painful joy.
'Tis a human thing, love, a holy thing, to
love what death has touched.

Chapter 24

Death Be Not Proud

AFTER ROGER'S DEATH, I was even more convinced about what Granny shared with me many times beneath the sycamore tree was true. Granny said God always placed someone in your path for a reason and that we had to discern who they were and their purpose because they were there to guide you to your purpose. That was so profoundly true. I had been living my life day by day trying to make the right decisions; imperfect as I knew I was, I knew that Roger was on my path for a reason. He affirmed for me something my Pops always told me, and that was to believe in your potential unapologetically. I also knew Patek was on my path because she was the sound of reason, and she had really earned the status of a true friend. We supported each other in good and bad times. I also believed in my heart that George was placed on my path because he always wanted me to become successful. We grew up together with pure friendship and ambitions; we became friends and now lovers and companions. I decided I would stay on at Roger's until the end of April in order to help the staff make the transition to the new boss, Roger's son. Staff was still grieving his death, and you could feel it every time you entered that space.

One day, we sat in the office for lunch as everyone ordered up food. As we sat at the table, everyone talked about what they would always remember the most about Roger. Near the end of the conversation and before everyone had finished lunch, I thought this would be the appropriate time to let them know I had given notice to leave at the end of the month. When I did, Andrea and Pete were cut-ups. "Well," Andrea gushed out, "so who are you going to work for?"

I looked at her and started laughing profusely. Sarcastically, I responded, "Oh, I suppose I'll be working for myself, Andrea." At that moment, if only I could have taken a picture of her face as she looked at Pete, and he snapped his head like a bobblehead.

"Wow, well, good luck with *that*!" she exclaimed while rolling her eyes.

"Thank you, Andrea and Pete. I will really, really miss you two."

Everyone else seemed to be happy for me and congratulated me to boot. Without going through the details of my new venture, I just told them that I would be sending something to them about the new venture.

The month went very fast, and the goodbyes were sweet and solemn at the same time. But when I walked out the door, I walked with the confidence and knowledge needed to start on my new journey. I stopped by the market to pick up some wine, and I ran into Mete. He was shopping before going home as well. We spoke to each other, and I walked home. This walk home was different; it had a feel of an ending and a new beginning. Days following my exit, I spent most of my time working. I had a lot of time to think, and I thought about my favorite artist Van Gogh. I learned a lesson from him. Many people didn't know that he created more than nine hundred paintings and only sold one during his lifetime; Van Gogh, one of the most prolific painters in the world, died thinking he was a failure! I wanted to ensure that I used everything within my power to work smart, respect people, treat people fair, and be honest but experience some fruits of my labor. I always wanted my mom, Pops, and Granny to be proud of me. Every decision I made would determine if I could make myself proud as well. My Granny would always say, "When you make a decision, be sure that you can look yourself in the mirror with clear eyes the next day." I also watched my dad as he worked with diligence under tremendous pressure, prejudice, and racism with great respect for time; he valued it.

Three weeks went by, and my business had a great start. August had come around again. Anatasie called with the fabulous news that I had paid off Jean Claude's investment with interest. She also told me she had received a phone call from Roger's attorney and that I was extended an invitation to a meeting at his office. The meeting was held in Paris in lieu of Toulouse.

A day later, I jumped a taxi. When I arrived and the moment I stepped off the elevator, I was escorted into a conference room and sat at this long mahogany table where I saw Roger's family and Latecia as well. It finally hit me; this is the reading of Roger's will. The attorney introduced everyone sitting at the table. This would be the first time I'd met Roger's son; his companion was there and ex-wife Andree as well. It seemed odd that Latecia and I would be the only nonfamily members present. The attorney started reading what was bequeathed to family members. I sat there with my hand folded on the other on my lap beneath the table. When he called my name, he started read-ing about how much Roger liked my spirit and dedication, and as he was reading, I was kinda hearing and kinda still in amazement about why I was even there. At the end of the accolades, he said, "Roger bequeathed you the sum of fifty thousand dollars to be invested and restricted in your own business. The sole amount would be placed in a blind trust to be used in the development and support of your business." I teared up instantly, and the tears started to flow down my cheeks. So much so that they had to pass the tissue box over to Latecia and me as well.

It happened so quickly, signing papers and handshaking with the attorney and family members that were gracious. With each handshake, there were words of congratulations to Latecia and me. When we left and while riding on the elevator, Latecia and I held each other's hands. It was the longest elevator ride we'd ever taken. When the elevator finally stopped, we stepped out and gave each other a hug and chatted a bit, and we each hailed a taxi. In the taxi, I called Anatasie and shared the good news with her. When I got home,

I couldn't wait to call my dad with the news. I called, and there was no answer. I called my two brothers, no answer, and so I thought I would try one more person. I called Granny and no answer.

I undressed, threw on some sweats, walked down to the studio, and sat there for about twenty minutes. I tried calling my folks again without luck. I thought I wanted to share this with my family before I shared it with George, but I didn't realize and forgot that it was early in the States. There were a few things I could have done in the studio, so I spent some time following up on a few tasks. It was getting really late, and I thought I'd get up around 3:00 a.m. and call. After all, it would be 8:00 a.m. in the States. I sat the alarm and fell off to sleep.

The clock sounded at 3:00 a.m., and I rolled out of bed. I went for a drink of water and washed my face with cold water in order to wake up. I dialed my Pops, and finally someone answered. "It's about time somebody answered my call. Where have you guys been? I've been calling all of you." There was a long pause, and I thought I had disconnected. "Hello, Pops!"

Finally, my dad responded in a trembling voice, "Pumpkin," he said, "I've got some bad news. Your Granny has passed."

"What are you saying, Pops? That couldn't be true. I just spoke with her…"

"Pumpkin, she has been ill for some time now. We just did not want to burden you. She wouldn't let us burden you." I cried uncontrollably, and my dad kept saying, "I know, darling."

"What happened?" I asked. Pops said Granny had congested heart failure. "I've got to come home, Pops. I'll be there by Tuesday."

When I placed the phone on my bed, I literally just drowned myself in my tears. I could see Granny as though she were standing right next to me. When I finally fell off to sleep, I had this vivid dream about Granny and me sitting beneath the sycamore tree talking to me, but strangely enough, she kept fading into the trunk of the tree. As I kept pulling on her hand, she would touch mine as if to require I let go. When I woke up, I had cried so much a headache had made its way into my overcrowded brain. But nothing could match the ache in my heart. There was no remedy for that. I sat on the side of my bed for a while until I could find the strength to get up and run my bath water. Around 8:00 a.m., I called Anatasie and shared the grim news with her. She asked if there was anything she could do. We went over the immediate things that needed to be attended to in my absence. She asked me not to worry that things would be taken care of, and she made me aware she would contact my clients too. I called Patek and told her as well. She abruptly ended the call, and in five minutes, she was at my door. She let herself in and came straight to me and embraced me. She didn't say a word. When she stopped embracing, she went into action. She fixed tea, croissant, butter, and jam. She sat it at the small table in front of the window. I sat there with her, and we spoke no words. I cried uncontrollably. When we finished breakfast, she asked me what day I wanted to depart and if I wanted an open return date. She made the flight arrangements. When she finished that, she pulled my small luggage out and started packing for me. She came over to the window as I sat there in a daze and showed me items to give thumbs up or down for the luggage. She rearranged the bed covers, changed the sheets, and pulled the comforter back. She walked over and placed her hands on my shoulder and asked me to go to bed. I obliged. I walked over to the bed and got under the covers. She turned the lights down, turned on music, and sat for another hour or until I fell off to sleep and then left. I stayed in bed for two days until the day before leaving for the States. My nights were spent in complete darkness. I could hardly catch a breath when crying. Patek called to check on me and to hear what had happened to Granny.

On the day of my departure, Patek road to the airport with me, hugged me, and watched as I walked to the terminal.

We're on Our Own

ON THE FLIGHT to the States, I just kept thinking about Granny and wondering if this was a dream. I realized I had not called George, but I just couldn't yet. For seven hours, I kept going over and over in my brain why couldn't I detect something wrong with Granny. That weighed heavily on my mind. I started thinking if I had been so selfish that I had not detected any signs that I should have. I guess it was guilt. I flew into New Orleans, had a layover, and finally caught a flight to Jackson, Mississippi, airport. Coming through the terminals just seemed different this time. I went down to the baggage area to retrieve my luggage and to meet Pops. As I was walking through the terminal, I was thinking how selfish I was for forgetting that Granny was my dad's mother. I thought Pops must be devastated. At that point, I knew I had to muster up some courage and be supportive of Pops.

I reached the escalator to go down to the turnstile to retrieve my luggage. I walked and stood there waiting for the luggage to pass through. Finally, I saw mine and reached for it. I started outside to find Pops, but instead my brothers were there. Dobie waved me to the car and met me to grab my luggage. "Hi, sis, how was your flight?"

"It was okay, you know, seven hours to think," I answered. I was standing there while he placed my luggage in the car trunk. I waited to give him a hug. When he closed the trunk, I opened my arms, and we both collapsed in each other's arms, tearing. We both got in, and he started saying he couldn't believe Granny was gone. I had so many questions to ask. "Dobie, did you know she was sick?" I insisted.

"Granny never told us anything, but she would talk to Pops every night. He never went to bed without calling her. Pops had been driving to her place doing some work for her, so he saw her almost every other day. He said she insisted on not telling us. I really didn't know everything until Pops told us she was in the hospital. We went to visit her, and that's when we discovered the seriousness of her illness," Dobie explained. I told him I felt guilty because I was away doing my thing yet not checking in on Granny as much I should. Dobie assured me, "Lisa, even if you had, she wouldn't have let you know the extent of her illness. You know how Granny was. She was very independent, and she loved us too much to share that because she didn't want us to stop our lives." I supposed he was right, but it still didn't take the hurt from my heart.

"Where is Pops?" I asked.

"He's at the funeral home finishing the arrangements."

"What funeral home?" I inquired.

"The same one mama was in, People's Funeral Home."

We learned the family viewing of the body was the next night. Granny, being the person she was, had left instructions as to what to do all the way down to what she should be buried in. After arriving at Pops, I put away my things and fixed dinner for Pops and my brothers.

I decided it was time to call George. I dialed his number, and he answered so happily. I hated to tell him the bad news, but he knew something was wrong. "Babe, my Granny died, and I'm in Mississippi for the funeral," I said in a shivering voice with tears flowing down my cheeks.

"Oh, sweetie, I am sorry to hear that. Was it sudden?" he asked.

"No, she had a brief illness, congested heart failure, and she passed several days ago."

"What can I do?" he asked. "I'll be there, Lisa. See you soon, okay?" This made me happy because I just did not want to fall apart. He reassured me of his love and hung up.

There were a few people who came over before Pops returned home. As I sat in the den in the dark, I kept hearing them talking about "the body." It just daggered me each time I heard it because I just couldn't fathom Granny—the vibrant, frisky, lovable woman— now being referred to as the body. I closed the door and fell asleep waiting for Pops. Someone shook me to wake me up, and it was Pops. "Hi, Lisa, how are you, darling?"

I just let it all hang out; I cried and was visibly shaken. "How are you doing, Pops?"

He started to console me by letting me put my head on his shoulder as we sat on the couch in the den. "I miss her too, darling, and I'm hurt, but I thank God every day that I spent some quality time with her. She would want you to think of her that way, not to have any regrets."

"I know, Pops, but it hurts so badly." I cried.

It seemed death had visited Pops within three months because Johnny Ray passed as well. Pops shared with me that Johnny Ray told him about what he had done to me and asked for forgiveness. "I told him I was not the one he should be asking for forgiveness. I'm sorry you went through that, Lisa, and I wished you had told me because I would have handled it. It was hard for me to forgive him, but I certainly won't forget it," Pops said.

"Pops, I didn't tell you because I knew you would take care of him, so I just made sure I had less chances of being around him. That's why I was glad you allowed me to go with you to work. That was my way of handling it," I stated empathically.

Thirty minutes later, I got up, washed the dishes, and put them away. When I turned the lights out, I headed for the bedroom, and I laid across the bed in my grief until I fell asleep. The next morning, the phone rang, it was Patek inquiring about how I was doing. I thanked her and told her I would be okay. Then I got a call from George to check in on me as well. He would be in Jackson at his relatives tomorrow, as the funeral was the day afterward. At 2:00 p.m., it was time for family to view Granny at the funeral home. When we arrived, just passing through where others lay in order to get to the chapel where Granny lay was heart-wrenching. I stood in the back of the chapel vailed while watching as other family members viewed.

Finally, my Pops came and grabbed my hand and walked with me. When I looked at Granny, she looked so peaceful and content. She was my beautiful Granny, my soulmate, as we always shared something special beneath the sycamore tree. When I saw the peace on her face, it was the same safe and peaceful look I would see on her face when we sat beneath the tree. Granny would close her eyes and listen to every word I had to say. She would awake and lean against the trunk of the huge tree that abetted our gathering. It was that kind of peace that I saw in her face. I stepped away from the casket with some solace, some comfort in knowing she was at peace. From that point on, there were no tears for me, just thoughts about the time we spent together.

That evening, Pops asked me to represent the grands by speaking at the celebration of life. The day of the funeral, the funeral home attendants were more than professional and kind. They guided us through everything. Pops, Dobie, Billy, and I rode in the limo. The procession was lengthy. Granny knew a lot of people from her church, and they were there in groves. When we arrived at the church, I saw George. He walked over to me and joined me in the line. My brothers and father didn't say anything, but they were wondering who this white man was. I'd forgotten to tell them about George in the grieving process. He held my hand and walked with the family as we walked behind the casket. When it was time for me to speak, I stopped at the casket first. I walked to the pulpit: "I will miss you, Granny, so much at our special meeting place beneath the sycamore tree. It was beneath that tree that we converged so much of us. It was where you taught me to be a woman, Granny. I thank you for sharing that space with me, for the hundreds of lessons taught, and that many I have realized as a woman and have coped and survived because of you. I know, Granny, you will appreciate this quote I am going to recite in your honor by John Irving: *'When someone you love dies, and you're not expecting it, you don't lose her all at once; you lose her in pieces over a long time—the way the mail stops coming, and her scent fades from the pillows and even from the clothes in her closet and drawers. Gradually, you accumulate the parts of her that are gone. Just when the day comes—when there's a particular missing part that overwhelms you with the feeling that she's gone, forever—there comes another day, and another specifically missing part.'* 'I'll always love you, Granny. I will see you soon on the other side beneath the sycamore tree."

We listened to the many kind words people expressed. It seemed Granny's entire church members and neighbors spoke about her. I learned of her charitable efforts for young people and the poor. I learned she had sponsored a young girl name Rita from birth until her college days. Yes, Granny was who I thought she was.

The roughest time for me was at the gravesite. To throw a rose on the casket was too much finality. George squeezed my hand tightly, affirming he was there for me. He would give me tissues as I cried as well. After the gravesite activity, the repass was held at our house. Pops had it catered, as we were expecting people to drop in to give their condolences. Members of my Granny's church handled everything. I found a moment to introduce Pops and my brothers to George as we met in the den. "Pops, I'm sorry I hadn't told you about George. George, this is my Pops, my brothers Dobie and Billy. George is my boyfriend or significant other." And I smiled.

My brother Dobie said, "See, Pops? I told you she was holding out on us. She does have a boyfriend!"

I laughed, and they shook George's hand. Pops said, "I know you, don't I?"

George said, "You might, Mr. Harris, because you were the contractor for my granddad's work at his house. That's where I met Lisa," he explained.

"Oh yeah, I remember now. You were the young man that used to swim and talk with Lisa, right?"

"Yes, sir," responded George.

I left them talking as I watched Pops and George walk outside on the deck. I went to put on some comfortable clothes. When the house had emptied out with the guests and the women had cleaned everything, I sat on the deck with George. "George, you were sharing some news with me. What was it?" I asked.

"Oh, I wanted to tell you that my family decided to invest in my restaurant."

I told him that was great news, and I told him I had so much to share with him.

"So how long are you going to be here, sweetie?" he asked.

"I'll be here for a week or so, babe."

He asked me to travel with him to Chicago for a couple of days to meet his folks before flying back to France, and I agreed. When he left, I went into the den to talk with Pops. I sat next to him and laid my head on his shoulder. "So what did you think about George, Pops?"

He said, "Lisa, I was a little surprised, but not because he was white but that you had a boyfriend, period!"

We both laughed. I told him I had shared my happiness with Granny, and I got her blessings. He asked me if I was prepared to deal with what comes with an interracial relationship. "Pops, I suspect there is going to be a lot of pushbacks, but the only thing I can do is to manage our relationship wherein we are secure with each other's love. You noticed I said we, right?"

Pops nodded his head and replied, "Yep, Lisa, it's some cruel people out here both black and white that won't approve of this. Just be prepared."

"That's a conversation George and I had. I wanted him to understand my expectations of him, and I wanted to know his intentions as well."

"I love you, and I don't want you to be hurt by some bullshit, understand?"

"Yes, Pops," I responded. "I love you, Pops!"

He hugged me and said, "I love you more, pumpkin."

The next two days, I learned that Granny had left her house to me and the old truck to boot. I cherished the house and truck. I just needed to talk with Pops about what we could do with it. I spent some really quality time with my family for the next few days, and Pops and I had made a reasonable decision about the house.

We decided to fix it up and let it be the place family members could visit and chill from time to time. One thing I was clear about is that black Mississippians understood the value of property; they knew you never give it up or sell it away. Pretty much, it went back to slavery—you know, the forty acres and a mule thing.

On Friday, George and I left Jackson for Chicago. We landed at O'Hare Airport around 5:00 p.m. I did not know what to anticipate, but I knew it would be an event. I had reserved a hotel room at the Drake in downtown Chicago even though George wanted me to stay over at his parents' house in Lincoln Park. George dropped me off in the taxi. I checked in, and once I was settled in, I told George I would take a taxi over to visit with him and his parents for dinner later that evening. In the meantime, I decided to just go for a walk in Chicago and to look at the fashions as well. Chicago was beautiful to walk around at dusk. Since I was only a block or so away from the stores on Michigan Avenue and the Gold Coast, I decided to go for a stroll. It was a brisk Chicago wind but a nice autumn day in September, so I bundled myself up and walked for a while. Chicago's skyline was so beautiful, as we flew over the lake on the way in, and once on the ground, I could see its beauty more clearly. I glanced through the windows of Burberry, Bvlgari, and Channel. I had to admit that American windows were different from French. American retailers put it all up front, and Parisian retailers enticed you into the stores without a lot of fluff.

I returned to the hotel and took a shower. I dressed and sat at the desk, writing a note in my planner. There was a knock at the door, and it was George. He was so excited. He helped me with my wrap, and we walked to the elevator, holding hands where he sneaked a kiss. We took a taxi to his parent's house and walked up to a three-flat red brick building. George unlocked the door to a very eloquent step-down living room with very conservative decor but lovely. George belted out, "I'm home, guys!" They were all in other parts of this huge seven-bedroom home.

I heard a voice, "We're in the kitchen. Come on in!"

Holding hands, we walked down this long hallway, passed two bedrooms, two bathrooms, and finally to a wide open-space kitchen with a marbled top island at least twelve feet long. All white faces were sitting around the island, chatting. If I could have snapped a picture for keeps, that would have been the one to snap. It was obvious they were not expecting me to be black. Once they resocked their eyeballs, they spoke cordially. Now the curiosity was setting in. His mom stepped up to say hello with a weak handshake, and the others followed with strong handshakes introducing themselves. George made a formal introduction, "Lisa, this is part of my family. Family, this is Lisa." His father came to me and gave me a hug and gave up his seat at the long kitchen island; George pulled up a stool next to me and immediately put his arm around me on the stool.

For a while, there was some comfortable chatter. His uncle and his father's brother were a hoot. He just had no filter on his mouth. It appeared, while he was successful, he was the real one in the family besides George. He might have been deemed as the "white sheep" of the family. His father, Jim, was unassuming and quiet, but he definitely was a talker. "Lisa happens to be in the states because her grandmother passed," he shared. They gave their condolences sincerely, and I graciously accepted. His mother, Alexia, came back in the kitchen to let us know that dinner was served.

"It's about time. How long has it been?" touted Uncle Larry.

Everyone brushed him off and grabbed their glasses and followed Alexia. We walked down a long hallway to an open atrium where this huge dining room table was eloquently set and two servers were waiting to serve guests. I was so happy to see that the servers were white because that would have thrown my entire day. George sat next to me and his uncle next to him; he had cousins as well sitting around the table. As soon as we sat down, I took my napkin and placed it on my lap, elbows and hands off the table. The servers came around with our choices to drink. I had a glass of sangria and water. It was a typical Greek dinner. There were charcoal-grilled and spit-roasted meats with souvlaki, chunks of skewered pork, calamari, whole baked fish, potatoes, fasolada, and a white-bean soup. There was plenty of food and, of course, plenty of desserts. I ate politely because I really didn't have an appetite.

After dinner, George and I walked to the back where there was a patio area and deck. We were alone finally. We sat, and I leaned over with my head on his shoulder. I started telling George about how well the business was doing and about the gift I received from Roger. He was overwhelmed with joy. I loved the quiet and hugs from him. We visited for a while, and before leaving, Alexia asked if I would meet her for lunch the next day. I agreed since it would be our last day in town. George and I left for the hotel, and Alexia asked George if he would be returning. He looked at her with the strangest look, like "stay out of my business" kind of look. He said, "Maybe, maybe not, Ma. It depends on Lisa."

I looked and shook her hand and said, "It was nice to have met you, and the meal was fantastic."

With her weak shake, she said, "Sure, Lisa, it was nice meeting you as well. I look forward to our lunch tomorrow. I'll call you with where tomorrow morning, okay?"

I said thanks, and George and I walked away holding hands. We said our goodbyes to the others and left. When we returned to the hotel, we both were totally exhausted. We went to bed spooning all night. When I awakened, George had gone. He left a note to let me know he had to meet his uncle at his office to finalize the investment agreement. Alexia rang the room around 10:00 a.m. to let me know we would be eating at Diana's Opaa and asked if I wanted her to pick me up. I politely said, "No, thanks, I will meet you there. I'm looking forward to it." I arrived ten minutes before time and sat comfortably, waiting for Alexia. When she arrived, the waiter showed us to a table. I ordered a sangria wine and Greek salad; she did the same. I was saying to myself, *Here we go, Lisa.* She started, "Oh, it was nice meeting you, Lisa, as George talked about you so much. He never told me how you guys met."

"We met years ago in Mississippi during his visit with his grandfather. Your father was a client of my Pops."

She looked, shaking her head. "Oh my," she said. "So you two have known each other for some time?"

"Yes," I quickly said. "When we both went off to college, we started writing to each other, but we both became so very busy until we lost contact until last year."

The questions kept coming, and I kept being vague. Then she said, "We were so disappointed George decided not to go to law school because there are generations of legal eagles in our family. We just couldn't understand why he didn't want to pursue his law degree," I said,

"I see. George pretty much has always had a passion for the culinary arts. He is very good at it as well."

"What do you have a passion for?" she inquired.

I didn't know for a second if she was trying to be sarcastic or sincere. "Oh, I have many passions. Professionally I love what I do. I am a designer, and I love the business. I have a passion for my family, and of course, I have a passion for George." And then I smiled.

"May I ask you what your intentions are as far as George?"

I said to myself, *There it is.* Here is the typical white privileged woman who thought I wanted something from her son—want something as in he got money and maybe I didn't, as in maybe her son was going too low beneath her expectations to date. I looked at her as I sat up straight and said, "My intentions are the same as George's intentions. As a matter of fact, he expressed his intentions to my father while he was in Mississippi. Both our intentions are to love each other unconditionally, to support each others' ambitions, to become a great chef and me a great businesswoman, and to grow together."

"So you have your own business?"

"Yes, as a matter of fact, I do, and it's doing more than great."

She quickly said, "I come from a generation wherein the man takes care of the woman, so I was just wondering—"

I cut her off in midsentence. "I don't come from that type of DNA. I've always been taught by my Granny and father as well that I can be whatever I want to be, and I can carve my own path, and that's exactly what I've done. I can't fathom what it must be like to rely on someone else. For us, that is George and I. We have our separate interests, but George understands what my expectations are for him as a man and for me to be a woman and reciprocal. So for your generation, that may have been the goal, but to me, that is like depending on someone to make my happiness when I know that I don't rely on anyone to do that, not even George. He adds to my happiness. You know what I mean?" I asked. "Is there a problem here?"

She replied, "No, I love my son, and I want him to be happy."

"Well, are you implying he isn't happy, or have you had this conversation with him at all?" I vehemently asked.

"No, we haven't spoken—"

I cut her off and said, "Then perhaps you should speak with George, but if it is something you want to tell or ask me, now is that time."

She sat and looked at me intensely and then gave a fainted smile. When she had finished that long diatribe, her face was flushed because she knew she had been read for filth. For the remainder of the lunch, it was general chitchat about her tennis league and her volunteer works as well. I obliged her. When the lunch ended, I shook her hand and thanked her for inviting me to lunch. I paid the tip for the wait staff. She gave me a light hug, and I caught a taxi back to the hotel. Later on that night, my babe came over, and we spent a lovely time together. When he asked me about the lunch with his mom, I assured him it went very well. I never shared the conversation I had with his mother. I did, however, have a feeling that George had cut the umbilical cord, and it would be tested going forward. I believed that conversation with Alexia was a conversation we might revisit down the road.

Chapter 26

Two Plus Two

WE RETURNED TO Paris together. On the flight back home, I had so much to think about. Realizing I had to go through the stages of grief, I wanted to ensure that it did not tank the things I needed to focus on like my own health, my ability to think with clarity about my business, and my relationship with George. And most importantly, I wanted to have people in my space that would not allow me to self-loath about Granny's death. I had great comfort knowing that Patek was in my life and George too because they would hold me accountable. George spent two days with me and headed for Provence to start his exit strategy for developing his business. We had this great conversation about what we wanted to do going forward. We both knew that our relationship could very well be tested with careers soaring upward. George and I had to set some boundaries both personally and professionally; that would allow us to step back from it all and make time for us.

Three months later in the December of 1985, I opened up my own fashion house with ten employees in Paris. My clients grew from the initial twenty-five premier clients to fifty clients. I was excited to be doing a public showing at the next fashion week. Patek finally decided to open up her long-awaited gallery via Jean Claude's financing. Amanda's fashion house in Milan was fully functional and successful. We would partner on projects, and we worked together to refer clients to each other. George identified a property in Paris not too far from the Eiffel Tower and launched his restaurant Chez Gormon. The restaurant was doing great and had received very welcoming reviews from the food critics.

In our personal life, we remained committed to consistently courting each other to keep our relationship fresh. We sustained our date nights and took trips together when possible. George placed an invite on my work desk early that morning to meet him at the restaurant for our weekly date night at the end of the last shift and at the closing that Wednesday. I always looked forward to those nights because it was undoubtedly the most precious time for us to sit and focus on just us. I could always discern if he had a great day because he would have a glow about himself. If it was not a good day, he would always say at the beginning of our one-hour shoptalk, "We keeping plugging, right?" This night, he mentioned our anniversary date was coming up in eight months, and he wanted to plan something for us. Usually, I did the planning. I was more than willing to relinquish to him. Who was I to deny him that; I said yes!

"What did you have in mind, babe?" Our evening as usual went without problems and us being called out to handle anything. That I asked.

"Oh, I will come up with something, I'll check your calendar before I plan anything, okay?"

"That's fair," I quipped.

After dinner, we decided to walk because the weather in that moment granted the opportunity. Even in the night, Paris shined. It started to rain a little, and when the shower was done, raindrops still wanted to cling falling one drop at a time; that was confirmation that it was spring in Paris. The rain always brought with it a somewhat hazy view, and if you're walking down the Champs, you could barely see the old gray arch. As we walked through Paris, we noticed the growing greenery around the city and the sounds of people enjoying one another's company. Parisians knew how to take time to enjoy and savor moments. Over the years living in Paris, I learned how to cultivate and embrace those moments as well. While walking, I was always aware when he had a thought because he would squeeze my hand and look at me passionately. No words said, no words needed to be spoken.

Eight months later in August, George and I found ourselves on the road in a car to the south of France to celebrate our anniversary. A lot had changed since we were together in the south of France. We were older; I was twenty-eight and he was thirty. He would not tell me what or where we were going. All the way there, we listened to our favorite jazz we both loved. Like the first time I went to the south of France, we stopped to get petro and for me to pee. I bought some jelly beans, as I had done the years before, for us to munch on. I separated them by feeding him the red ones. I liked the purple. I began to recognize we were again headed for Haut Var, the tiny little town that packed a big punch for us. It was where George and I first made love and made a commitment to each other. I also noticed we were going to a different location. When we pulled up to this place, it looked like a country church but more than a church. The church-like structure looked as though it came straight out of poet Thomas Gray's poems. It was quaint, sitting in the middle of a patch of greenery. It was the stone-white brick that struck me aesthetically, so clean and pristine. At the top of the church, there was this huge black bell that served as a perfect contrast with the whiteness of the building. I felt like I had escaped through a time wormhole to another century. Such beauty was almost impossible.

I was thinking, *Wow, here is another unique gem George has found.* He ran around the car and offered his hand to assist me out of the car. I placed my hand confidently in his, and we both walked the tiny steps of the church-like cottage. He had the keys, and so he opened the door. When he opened the doors, we walked down what looked like a runway, but it was the aisle, and I had an aha moment; it was actually a church. When we reached the altar, quickly from the wings of the church, I saw my Pops, my brothers, and George's parents and uncle walking toward us. When I looked at George, he was just showing that million-dollar smile. "George, what's going on?" I asked emphatically.

My Pops and brothers said hi, and George's parents said hi. George got down on one knee, and I almost lost it. He had it all planned. "Lisa, I have already asked your father for your hand. You and I have gone through a lot together, and we have grown together as well. You are my queen. I love and respect you, and you are my best friend. Will you marry me?"

My knees almost buckled, but I was able to respond and say, "Yes, I will marry you, George."

Everyone clapped as he placed the most beautiful ring on my finger. My Pops and brothers hugged my neck; his parents said congratulations, and his dad hugged my neck well. His mom gave a warm cordial hug as well. That wasn't all of it! He said, "I'm just going to make a suggestion, but only if you agree. I am prepared to marry tonight on our anniversary."

My eyes were about to jump out of my sockets. I said, "Babe, I don't have a dress, I don't have shoes—"

He stopped me in midsentence and asked, "Do you trust me?"

I said yes. I looked, and behind me out came Patek, Donnie, Greg, and Amanda with everything in hand. "You have everything you need, so are you ready, sweetie?"

I embraced him and said yes.

"Then come on and get dressed!"

They escorted me to a dressing area in the back of the church. The gals Donnie and Greg went into action. They made my face and did my hair. Amanda teared as she pulled out the most beautiful dress in the world that she had designed—my wedding dress. Patek had shopped to select a pair of Roger's beautiful pumps. They went to get dressed, as they were my bridesmaids. I couldn't wait to see whom George chose for his best man and groomsmen. While in the dressing area alone, there was a knock at the door, and I asked them to come in. It was Pops. He looked so nice in his tuxedo. He hugged my neck, and then he gave me two gifts for something borrowed and something blue. First, he gave me a blue pendant that was my mom's, and he placed it around my neck; and then something borrowed, a beautiful garter with blue and white ruffles that was my Granny's. He said, "Your Granny always thought about your future. She gave me this a year ago and told me I would know when to give it to you." He kissed me on my forehead and told me how proud he was of me and that he loved me. I teared up, and he handed me a tissue to wipe my tears. "You look like your mother. You are a beautiful bride, pumpkin."

When he left the room, I pulled myself together. My two maids of honor, Patek and Amanda, escorted me to a holding area, and they prepared to walk in before me. When I heard the violins, it was surreal. Amanda and Patek walked in first, and then I heard the wedding march. As I walked down the aisle, the small chapel had garnered more people. Many of my coworkers, Andree, Jean Claude, and some of my clients were seated in the seats, Paul and Kem. I looked to see whom George had chosen as his best man, and wouldn't you know, Uncle Larry. His cousins were there as grooms-men. Many of his employees were there sitting with his family members. I saw my brothers and their wives, Mr. Wilford and his wife from New York, Donnie and Greg and their companions, along with Patek's boyfriend; Mete was even there. My heart was heavy. When I made it to the altar, the pastor went through the wedding vows that were not traditional at all, and that made me happy. The "to honor and obey" was taken out. I was trembling and afraid I would forget to recite the vows correctly. After we exchanged vows, we kissed, and we were married!

Everything else was planned. Someone drove us to a beautiful, decorated French chateau that had the most beautiful open patio. There were lavender and white lights streamed all over. Lavender flowers as centerpieces dawned long white tableclothed tables with candles and beautiful glassware. The servers stood around the room, waiting to get into action. The wedding party was seated first. The reception was absolutely phenomenal. When it was time for the dance with my Pops, I could see the joy in his eyes. He danced and looked like a proud papa. Then the dance with my babe was next. We found our way into the center of the dance floor, and the band leader introduced the guest performer for the evening and the special song he would sing, "And now to the bride and groom." And the DJ played our favorite song, "You Were Meant for Me." Wow! This was too much to take in. When we heard Donnie Hathaway's "You Were Meant for Me," I placed my head in my husband's chest as we both understood the gravitas of the lyrics. We looked in each other's eyes and proclaimed our love for each other. "Did I plan well, sweetie?" he asked.

"Yes, babe, you did. I am so happy."

The night went by, and happiness was in the air. All guests danced the night away. I looked over across the room and saw George's family congregating with my family. His father was talking with mine, and Alexia was talking with my sisters-in-law. The food was the best, as George wouldn't have had it any other way. He and I left the reception first, and we were driven to our special place in Haut Var. My wedding night was the most beautiful experience and the most intimate lovemaking we had ever experienced, and it's impossible to share. I was now a wife, and George was my husband.

The next day, we all met for breakfast at the same place where the reception took place. Following the breakfast, everyone went in their own directions. Our folks took a train back to Paris together, where they would spend another week for vacation. A myriad of things happened over the two-week visits. I had a chance to spend a couple of days with my folks. They came by my shop, and my Pops was so proud. I did measurements for my Pops and brothers because I wanted to design suits for them. I took my sisters-in-law shopping, and they had the best time of their lives. Those ladies could shop without tiring, but they never knew I hated shopping because I never ever let on to them that I didn't. My in-laws visited my shop and were impressed. I went out to dinner with both our families at our restaurant, and it was great to see the smiles on their faces. The smiles on their faces were the result of observing for the first time George's passion. The next day, both families departed back to the states.

The following year in September 1986, George and I bought a two-bedroom condo in Paris, and we moved in. We had an interior decorator do the decor. We loved our new place! A week later, I met George at the restaurant for our Wednesday night dinner date. I told him I had a surprise for him. He came from the back of the restaurant into our private space lit with candles as we sat near a window. We had a great view of the Eiffel Tower, and the weather gods cooperated because it was a crystal-clear night. We could see the twinkling lights from the tower. After we ate dinner, I gave him a box to open. He was so curious. When he pulled out the contents of the box, he jumped up screaming. In his hand were two items: two tiny booties, one blue and one pink.

The End

About the Author

MONTIE R. APOSTOLOS is a senior fellow with the Academy for Urban School Leadership. She is the author of Fret Not Thyself, a memoir. She serves as an education consultant and teacher. She is also the Chicago publicist for Jewell Loyd, a WNBA Seattle Storm basketball star. She is the executive director of the Loyd Foundation. She was former school administrator for School District 65 in Evanston, Illinois, and Waukegan School District 60. Before that, she was an administrative account manager with Weber Shandwick Public Relations Firm in Chicago. In that capacity, she worked with more than six account managers whose clients included Campbell Soup, "Got Milk?" campaign, Harley Davidson, and Kraft Inc. She joined the agency with extensive management and communications experience, including twenty years of senior-level fundraising and ten years of corporate communications experience.

Prior to joining Weber Shandwick, Apostolos served as the divisional training and policy manager for Proffitt's Inc. Saks Fifth Avenue southeastern region. Other work experiences include working as a publicist for WLS-TV channel 7 (ABC) in Chicago and press assistant for the former Illinois state comptroller Roland Burris of Illinois during his first-term candidacy. She has consulted for a diverse number of not-for-profit institutions and organizations including PUSH for Excellence Educational Foundation, Northeastern Illinois University Foundation, and the Jackie Robinson Foundation Scholarship, to name a few. She has senior-level management experience at five major not-for-profit institutions and associations in Chicago that includes working as a development director and regional project manager for the College Fund Inc., development director for the Christian Action Ministry (CAM), resource development director for the Midwest Women's Center, special events coordinator for the Chicago Urban League, and director of marketing and public relations for the Illinois Parks and Recreation Association.

She has coordinated several events for clients including the NBA pro basketball Classic, Michael Jordan's Carlsbad benefit golf tournament, the College Fund's Parade of Stars television fundraising special; Walk Illinois, Mississippi African American Heritage Festival, Mississippi Gospel Festival, and Northeastern Illinois Foundation's "An Evening with Nancy Wilson" scholarship benefit, to name a few. She is a frequent motivational speaker for the Chicago public schools and major universities. She's been the keynote speaker and workshop facilitator at the University of Illinois Chancellor's Teachers Academy, Academy for Urban School Leadership, George Armstrong School of International Studies, Lake Forest College, and the Illinois Reading Council. She is a board member of the Loyd Foundation, Agape Youth Foundation, and Pegasus Theater. She was selected "Who's Who" in education in 2007, 2011, and 2021 by Biltmore and Strathmore's Who's Who Worldwide. She's been featured in the Chicago Tribune, detailing her experience as a change agent for Chicago public schools and model for NCLB school laboratory. She is a member of Delta Sigma Theta Sorority Inc.